The
BLOODY
SPUR

MICKEY SPILLANE
AND
MAX ALLAN COLLINS

The
BLOODY
SPUR

k

KENSINGTON BOOKS
http://www.kensingtonbooks.com

KENSINGTON BOOKS are published by

Kensington Publishing Corp.
119 West 40th Street
New York, NY 10018

All Kensington titles, imprints, and distributed lines are available at special quantity discounts for bulk purchases for sales promotion, premiums, fund-raising, educational, or institutional use.

Special book excerpts or customized printings can also be created to fit specific needs. For details, write or phone the office of the Kensington Special Sales Manager: Attn. Special Sales Department. Kensington Publishing Corp, 119 West 40th Street, New York, NY 10018. Phone: 1-800-221-2647.

Kensington and the K logo Reg. U.S. Pat. & TM Off.

Library of Congress Card Catalogue Number: 2017951256

ISBN-13: 978-1-61773-598-1
ISBN-10: 1-61773-598-1
First Kensington Hardcover Edition: February 2018

eISBN-13: 978-1-61773-599-8
eISBN-10: 1-61773-599-X
First Kensington Electronic Edition: February 2018

10 9 8 7 6 5 4 3 2 1

Printed in the United States of America

For Bob Randisi,
who has gunned down more bad men
than all the shootists put together

"Tomorrow is the most important thing in life.
Comes into us at midnight very clean.
It's perfect when it arrives
and it puts itself in our hands.
It hopes we've learned something from yesterday."
John Wayne

JOHN WAYNE AND MICKEY SPILLANE: A FRIENDSHIP

Mickey Spillane's famous crime novels—in particular those featuring his breakthrough character, Mike Hammer—are often discussed in terms of their violence and sexual content, which seemed so revolutionary in the late 1940s and early '50s. The sex seems almost tame these days, but the violence still packs a punch that Sam Peckinpah likely envied.

What more insightful commentators have always known is that the Mike Hammer stories are at heart about friendship and loyalty—the detective is almost always seeking the murderer of a friend, with an "eye for an eye" on settling that score. Most famously, in *I, the Jury* (1947), Hammer goes after the killer of his friend Jack Williams, his buddy in the Pacific who lost an arm while taking a Japanese bayonet blow meant for Mike.

Also central to the novels are Hammer's friendship with Captain Pat Chambers of Homicide and the detective's evolving relationship with his secretary Velda, who becomes the love of his life over the course of the decades-spanning series.

Similarly, many of John Wayne's films, particularly the

Westerns, explore themes of friendship and loyalty, from *Stagecoach* (1939) and its lawman who gives the Ringo Kid a chance to settle a score before taking him in, to *The Man Who Shot Liberty Valance* (1962), where Wayne's Tom Doniphon grants James Stewart's Ranse Stoddard a sense of manly accomplishment that perhaps he doesn't deserve. Other examples of friendship-driven yarns litter the Duke's filmography: Sheriff John T. Chance helping his deputy Dude find redemption in *Rio Bravo* (1959); Deputy U.S. Marshal "Rooster" Cogburn showing affection and even admiration for young Mattie Ross in *True Grit* (1969); and Ethan Edwards coming to accept half-breed surrogate son Martin Pawley in *The Searchers* (1956), perhaps the greatest Wayne Western, and the great John Ford's best film.

In real life, both Spillane and Wayne were loyal to a core group of friends, in Mickey's case fellow scribes like Dave Gerrity and Joe Gill, and in Wayne's such fellow Hollywood denizens as director John Ford and actor Ward Bond. And for a time, in the 1950s, a non-Hollywood denizen named Spillane was part of Wayne's inner circle.

When Mickey was at his early '50s peak, Wayne and producing partner Robert Fellows thought the best-selling, publicity-attracting writer was a natural, and starred him in the circus picture *Ring of Fear* (1954) as his famous mystery-writer self turned amateur sleuth. After several weeks of filming, Wayne was happy with Spillane the actor, but not so happy with the initial footage, and asked Mickey to rewrite the picture for extensive reshoots to be helmed by famed director William Wellman.

For *Ring of Fear* (available on DVD), Mickey declined either a screen credit or payment for his rewrite. Wayne had seen Mickey admiring a white Jaguar convertible in a Los Angeles showroom and had the snazzy vehicle delivered, wrapped in a red ribbon, to the writer's home in New-burgh, New York, with a card signed, "Thanks – Duke."

The John Wayne/Mickey Spillane friendship included the writer attending screenings to provide input when-ever the mystery writer happened to be in Hollywood. It also included one more occasion for Wayne to call upon Mickey's services as a screenwriter.

The correspondence in Mickey's files is unclear as to who initiated the project, but Wayne certainly expressed his enthusiasm for a Spillane Western. "The Saga of Calli York" (as it was originally titled) was intended for Wayne himself, Mickey told me, commissioned by the actor; but it's also possible that Wayne might have handed "York" off to some other appropriate star, per-haps Randolph Scott, Glenn Ford or Robert Mitchum, leads of various Wayne-produced films of the era.

Around when Mickey would have sent in his screen-play, Batjac—Wayne's production company—was deal-ing with the out-of-control budget, and ensuing box-office disappointment, of *The Alamo* (1960). While Batjac eventually rebounded, Wayne spent several years making pictures for other producers and various studios, which would have relegated "York" to a back burner.

Mickey and Bob Fellows, Wayne's ex-producing part-ner, went on to collaborate on two films, *The Girl Hunters* (1963) and *The Delta Factor* (1970), both from Spillane novels. The latter film proved a disappointment, both artistically and financially, but *The Girl Hunters* (now on DVD and Blu-ray) did respectable business and, with Spillane himself playing Mike Hammer and cowrit-ing the screenplay, has gone on to cult success. Mickey's performance in *The Girl Hunters* also inspired his self-spoofing series of long-running Miller Lite commercials of the 1980s and '90s.

Mickey would often speak fondly of Wayne and—while not one prone to expressing regrets—obviously wished the "York" project had come to light. Mike Hammer, he insisted, was a modern-day Western hero: "He wore the black hat, but he did the right thing."

Shortly before his death in 2006, Mickey indicated to his wife, Jane, that I should be given his files and asked to complete various unfinished projects—an honor that staggers me to this day. I was lucky to be one of the writers whom Mickey counted as a friend, and that you are holding this book in your hands tells you what kind of friend he was—and, for that matter, *is*—to me. Among the manuscripts entrusted were a dozen Hammer novels in various stages of development, several other unfinished crime novels, and a handful of movie scripts, including "York."

The Legend of Caleb York, published in 2015 by Kensington Books, is based upon Mickey's unproduced screenplay. Editor Michaela Hamilton—herself a longtime Spillane fan—has asked me to continue the saga of Caleb York, drawing upon various drafts of the screenplay and notes in Mickey's files.

Mickey provided York with a rich backstory as a Wells Fargo agent, which I may yet explore; but my wife, Barb (my collaborator on the "Trash & Treasures" mysteries), suggested that I might be best advised to explore further the characters, conflicts, and world Mickey created in his screenplay in any immediate sequels. *The Big Showdown* (2016) was the first such sequel, and *The Bloody Spur* is the second.

As was the case with the previous two Caleb York novels, picturing John Wayne in the lead is allowed but not required. My personal casting call would include (appropriately aged) Randolph Scott, Joel McCrea, Audie Murphy, James Garner, and Clint Eastwood. Wayne's protégé, James Arness of *Gunsmoke* fame, also makes sense. Perhaps from this list you might assume that Mickey and I, while hoping not to insult the intelligence of purists, are interested most in the mythic West.

You would be right.

Pardner.

Max Allan Collins

CHAPTER ONE

Being dead, Caleb York had come to realize, had its advantages.

When he'd ridden into Trinidad, New Mexico, six months back, York had been a stranger just passing through. For a year or more, the rumor had spread far and wide that the celebrated Wells Fargo detective had been gunned down. That Caleb York had gone the way of all flesh, or at least the way of all gunfighters.

That rumor had given York a blessed anonymity. As his midthirties reared up ahead of him like a spooked horse, York had grown ever more tired of facing down gunnies who wanted to make a reputation at his expense. Too often, reckless men and sometimes boys sought to force a showdown with a living legend whose prowess with a handgun had forged a name for him that only the likes of Wyatt Earp, John Wesley Hardin, and Wild Bill Hickok might rival.

As it worked out, when he bumped up against corrupt Sheriff Harry Gauge, York found it necessary to step out of the blessed obscurity of a supposed dead man to deal with a patch of trouble. Now he was sitting in Gauge's chair behind a big dark wooden desk in the plank-floored office/jail with its two barred street windows, wood-burning stove, and rough-hewn table under a wall of wanted posters and a rifle rack. Wearing the badge of a sheriff whom York had been obliged to kill.

Caleb York was a big, lean man, with a jaw that stopped just short of jutting and reddish-brown hair barely touched with gray at the temples. His pleasant features were set in a rawboned, clean-shaven face with washed-out blue eyes peering out from a permanent squint.

When York rode in those many months ago, some had called him a dude, although his way with a gun—and his fists—made it unlikely he'd hear that denigration again. Truth be told, his mode of apparel *was* on the dudish side, although in his view—the view of a man who'd been heading for San Diego and a job with Pinkerton's when fate and the needs of Trinidad had waylaid him—he merely looked professional.

In the manner of Bat Masterson and other serious law enforcement officers, York wore a black coat and black cotton pants tucked in hand-tooled black boots; his shirt was a light gray, with pearl buttons, and the string tie was black. His black hat had a cavalry pinch; a gray kerchief was knotted at his neck. His preferred weapon, a Colt Single Action Army .44, he wore low on his right hip, about pants-pocket level, and he kept it tied down.

Right now, however, the black coat and hat were on wall pegs to his right, and the gun in its bullet-studded belt was curled up, as if a snake in slumber, on his desk before him. He was staring at it, wondering how many more years would have to pass before men could walk down a street not wearing one. He wondered if, when

law and order finally came to the land, lawmen themselves could go out unarmed. He'd read that such was the
practice in England.

As if in answer to York's unspoken question, his
deputy—Jonathan Tulley—burst in like a jolt of reality.
"*Sheriff!*" Tulley blurted.

The old desert rat, skinny and white bearded, swam in
his baggy canvas pants, though the badge-pinned BVD
top under blue suspenders fit close. His shotgun was over
one arm.

Then words tumbled out of the sun-creased face. "Get
yourself down to the Victory, Sheriff, in one hell of a hurry!
There's a kid down there shootin' up the place! Miss Rita's
fit to be tied, and there's folks cowering under tables like
skeered rats."

"What brought you to the Victory?" York asked, slow
and cool, reaching for his gun belt. "Why court temptation?"

The bowlegged town drunk had dried out when York
made it a prerequisite of the deputy post.

"That there *gunfire!*" Tulley yelped.

"You're armed." York was on his feet now, still behind
the desk, strapping on the gun belt. "You're paid to en-
force the peace."

"I know I am, but—"

York raised a finger, which stopped his deputy, and
glanced at the wall clock. "I have a meeting to get to over
at Harris Mercantile. The mayor says it's important, and
he's the man who hands out our pay envelopes."

York knew damn well what the meeting was about.
He'd seen the fleshy man with the fine frock coat step
from the stage this morning, wearing self-importance like
a cloak. He'd asked "Bull" Mason, the stagecoach whip,

who his passenger was, and Bull had made a face and said, "Railroad agent." To a stagecoach man, that was worse than a hostile Indian.

Tulley swallowed and staggered over as if he *had* been drinking. "You ain't follerin' me, Sheriff. This just ain't any kid. It's *Kid McCurdy*!"

Though no wanted poster bore McCurdy's name, the young gunslinger had made a name for himself in nearby Las Vegas, New Mexico, where he'd finally been run out of even that wild town after four killings "in self-defense."

Tulley leaned his free hand on the desk. If his eyes had been any wider, they'd have fallen out and bounced around like acorns shaken from a branch. "McCurdy says he won't *stop* till you come see him *personal*."

York came out from behind the desk and tied the leather string that kept his holstered weapon snug to his thigh. He reached for his hat but left his coat hanging, since it might restrict movement.

"Shot up the place, you say," York said. "Did he bust up the mirrors with his target practice? Shoot the liquor bottles to pieces? Splinter the chuck-a-luck wheel?"

Tulley deflated some. "Well, no. Jest fired two rounds in the ceiling, and then, when I stuck my head in, he said to come fetch you. Waving his gun around! That's why he come to Trinidad—to see *you*."

"And you did what he told you to. Here I thought you were on Trinidad's payroll."

Tulley shuffled in place. "Well . . . what else was I to do?"

York pointed toward the door. "Right now, you're to go down there to the Victory's rear door, off the alley," the sheriff said, "and keep the place covered. Should things get out of hand—like should this pup manage to shoot me dead—I'd appreciate you plugging him for me."

"In the *back*?"

"Or have him turn around first, if you don't mind maybe dying."

Tulley thought that over, nodded, said, "We'll do 'er your way," and scurried out.

York made a disgusted click in his cheek as he checked the action of the .44. Then he slipped the iron back into its well-oiled home.

The afternoon was cool and crisp—this was November—and the boardwalks of Trinidad were empty, though faces in the windows in storefronts and the living quarters above peered out in anticipation of witnessing gunplay. That made York smile just a little as he walked along, spurs singing a lazy little tune. Gunfire sent everybody inside, he knew, but now a good many citizens were peeking out in expectation of more.

He didn't judge them harshly. The three hundred or so souls who lived in Trinidad were decent enough people. The town existed to serve the surrounding ranch-land area, and the folk here were mostly shop owners and clerks, whose days were usually dull, each one indistinguishable from the last. Part of why York was pulling down a hundred a month, plus his cut of the taxes he collected, was that reputation of his. He was something of a tourist attraction, like the Alamo or the O.K. Corral. Everybody who came to Trinidad wanted a glimpse of Caleb York.

Some, like Andrew "Kid" McCurdy, wanted more than just a glimpse.

York pushed through the swinging batwing doors and saw the small figure pacing by the bar, a mug of beer nearby. The Kid's gun was holstered. That was good. That was half the battle. Still, the biggest thing about the boy was the long-barreled Colt army revolver, worn high, not tied down.

McCurdy was seventeen, eighteen, somewhere in there. He stood perhaps five feet eight and was skinny enough to look scrawny in the blue cavalry bib-front shirt and shapeless Levi's; his Montana-peak Stetson looked new. This was no cowpuncher. Stick slender though he was, the Kid had a baby face, round and stubbly, with a snub nose and tiny dark eyes set too far apart. Like that other famous Kid—Billy—this one had buck teeth.

Stupidity came off him like steam over coffee.

Around them—with York just inside the doors and the Kid over at the left, near the bar—the Victory was like a church without worshippers, that big, that quiet. The elaborate tin ceiling was home to kerosene-lamp chandeliers, while gold-and-black brocade rode the walls; the long, highly polished oak bar went on forever, with its mirrors and bottles of bourbon and rye, towels dangling for divesting mustaches of foam, an endless brass foot rail broken up by spittoons. No bartenders were visible—likely cowering down in back of their counter—and patrons were huddled under tables, shivering, brave cowboys and town folk alike.

The casino section of the place was empty, from roulette to wheel of fortune. One poker table had been abandoned mid-game. Several satin-clad darlings shivered under their own table down toward the end, near the little stage with its unattended upright piano.

Tulley was tucked back behind a wooden post, not far from where he'd come in off the alley. Shotgun high and ready.

As for the proprietress, the lovely dark-haired Rita

Filley—a slender but shapely woman in her twenties, in the nicest satin gown in the house—she cowered for no man. She had positioned herself across the wide room from the bar, near the staircase. She looked irritated, her arms folded on the impressive shelf of her bosom.

Her eyes were hooded as they traveled to York, as if to say, *About time!* Or possibly, *Will you please do something about this?* He gave her the barest glance of reassurance.

McCurdy's dark, wide-set eyes were already on him, cold, hard, yet there was nervousness around them, marbles in twitchy housings.

"You're *him*, ain't you?" McCurdy said. The voice was high pitched, squeaky, but alive with the kind of crazy that made people dead.

"I'm the sheriff," York said.

"You're Caleb York!"

"Sheriff York, yes. Can I help you, son? In a bit of a hurry. I have a Citizens Committee meeting to attend. They're the folks who passed an ordinance against firing off handguns in a public place. But seeing as you're just passing through, I can let that ride. If *you* ride."

Fists swung at the air. "You killed a pal of mine!"

"Sorry to hear it. What was his name?"

"You wouldn't even remember! His name wouldn't mean *nothin'* to the likes of you!"

"Try me."

York hadn't meant to call a bluff, but that was what he'd done, judging by how McCurdy couldn't summon the name of the pal York had killed.

The Kid's chin crinkled. "That's what I mean to do, York—*try* you."

And the boy planted his feet and faced the sheriff, a hand hovering above that cavalry .45.

"We have no score to settle, son."

Holding his hands up mid-chest, palms out, York took a few steps toward the Kid.

York said, "Nobody has to die this afternoon. Ride out and tell everyone how you faced down Caleb York, and how the big man was afraid to fight you."

"*Are* you afraid?"

"What do you think?" York sensed the Kid was about to go for the .45 and said, "*Stop!*"

The Kid did.

"This is a nice place," York said conversationally, nodding around. "Everybody in town likes it, the Victory. Folks like yourself, passing through, find it a surprising palace for a bump in the road like Trinidad."

The Kid's forehead furrowed. "What the hell does *that* have to do with the price of beans?"

An easy shrug from the sheriff. "I don't want to see this place shot up. I don't want Miss Filley, the owner, to lose a mirror. Do you know how long it takes to get a new mirror in from Denver?"

"No."

"I don't, either, but I bet it's a good while. And those hooch bottles along the counter, those don't come cheap. And this fancy wallpaper, if it got tore up by bullets—"

"*Damn it*, York! What the *hell*—"

Hands still up, as if in surrender, York said, "Let's step outside and do this in the street. Like the grown-ups. We'll face each other, and I'll even let you draw first." He raised his voice. "*Everyone hear that!* If this doesn't go my way, you're to let this boy ride out. This is a fight I personally sanction."

The Kid was grinning, but one eye had a tic going now.

York held open the door for the Kid, who edged over and, still facing the sheriff, slipped out on the wooden porch and went down the steps slow and careful and backward.

Tulley was at York's side now, as the sheriff still held open a single batwing door.

"Ye can't *mean* that, Sheriff," Tulley whispered, squinting.

York smiled out at the Kid, nodding, almost friendly, and whispered back, "Of course not. If this doesn't go my way, blow his head off his shoulders."

Tulley said, "Be a pleasure."

York, moving slow, almost casual, went down the steps. He might have been strolling out into the afternoon to enjoy the gentle breeze, but his eyes stayed tight on the Kid. This boy was dumb and foolhardy, and that was just the kind of person who wound up killing somebody like Caleb York.

York raised his hands again mid-chest, palms out, and approached the Kid.

"Okay, son. You position yourself down there by the Mercantile. I'll stay right where I am."

"*Hell no!* I'll stay here, and *you* go down there."

York shrugged. "Fine. Do I have your word you'll let me get that far?"

"You got my damn word! I don't mean to have it said I bushwhacked Caleb York."

"Of course not," York said, with that easy smile. "This will be a fair fight between two men of honor."

The forehead on the roundish face squinched in thought, as if these words needed interpretation. "Right," the Kid managed to say. "Fair fight. A duel. Like in olden times."

"Like in olden times. We best shake on it."

York held out his hand, and the boy immediately accepted it. Then York clasped hard and twisted harder. The bones breaking sounded like distant gunshots.

Then the Kid was on his knees and screaming at the sky.

York leaned down, plucked the big gun from the boy's holster like a dandelion, and handed it to a grinning Tulley, who had come rattling down the steps when he saw what his boss was up to.

With a hand on Tulley's shoulder, York said, "Go get Doc Miller. He'll have to set that hand." Then he crouched and faced the weeping would-be gunslinger. "We'll get you fixed up, son."

"You . . . you *bastard*!"

York shook his head. "That hand, though, it'll never be the same. Unless you're ambidextrous."

"Ambi . . . ambi what?"

"Unless you can shoot just as well with your left hand."

"'Course I can't, you miserable son of a bitch."

"Well, you can always go off and practice for six months or so. When you're good enough as a southpaw, you come look me up, hear?"

The friendly tone seemed to confuse the Kid, who had no apparent sense of irony.

Then York gripped the boy's shoulder, hard, hard enough to make him wince, despite the pain his broken hand was already providing. The eyes in the round bundle of tics that was Kid McCurdy's face looked at York, whose smile disappeared into cold nothing.

"But if you do," he said, "I *will* kill you. You get just this one pass."

York rose from his crouch, dusted his knees off, and waited for his deputy to bring the doctor. The boy was a whimpering pile of bony humanity who'd likely never had a worse day.

Or a better one.

CHAPTER TWO

Willa Cullen, the only female at the meeting of the Trinidad Citizens Committee, was in attendance at the sufferance of the men, who knew her blind father—however he might resent or even deny it—required her aid. She had, for example, driven the buckboard into town from the ranch this morning.

The young woman—she had just turned twenty-three—was a familiar tomboy sight in Trinidad, attired today, as she so often was, in a red-and-black plaid shirt and denims and stirrup-friendly boots, her golden hair up and braided in back in a fashion that, like her lovely features and tall, shapely frame, suggested her late mother's Swedish heritage. So did her cornflower-blue eyes in their long-lashed setting.

Seated with her in a semicircular arrangement of chairs at the back of Harris Mercantile was a group of citizens who included both local merchants and ranchers, their attire sharply distinguishing which was which. One of the latter, seated beside her, was the rather shrunken figure of her father, George Cullen.

The old man's eyes were white with lack of sight; his

flesh was gray from too much time indoors; his once powerful rawboned face was a sunken-cheeked memory of its former self; and his sunken chest, the same. He wore a now too-large gray shirt and a black-string affair that Willa had tied for him, and new-looking black trousers that, like their owner, didn't get outside much these days.

A blind rancher didn't ride herd on men or cattle; he delegated such responsibilities—in Cullen's case to Whit Murphy, the trusted foreman of the Bar-O. Even now Murphy was seeing to things out at the spread.

A wood-burning stove, with a modest, fragrant fire in its belly, separated the meeting from the front of the store, with its high shelves, scurrying clerks, and eavesdropping customers. Standing toward the rear of the meeting place, a notebook and pencil in hand, was Oscar Penniman, the editor and owner of the *Trinidad Enterprise*, the town's newly minted weekly newspaper. The small, slender newspaperman wore a sack coat, matching vest, trousers, and intense concentration on his narrow mustached face.

A table on a slightly elevated platform faced the attendees. There sat the Citizens Committee members in attire usually reserved for Sunday, with Mayor Hardy in the higher-backed chair at the center, where the circuit court judge would sit when a trial came to town.

Hardy's qualifications were limited largely to his good grooming—he was, after all, the town barber. A short, slight, otherwise unprepossessing individual, the mayor had slicked-back, pomaded black hair and a matching handlebar mustache, impressive if oversize for such a narrow face.

At Hardy's right was their host: heavyset, blond, less impressively mustached Newt Harris, fifty-some, in the medium brown suit and dark brown string tie he wore on such occasions. At the mayor's left was apothecary Clem Davis, a bug-eyed scarecrow of a man; and next to him, hardware-store owner Clarence Mathers, his muttonchops so massive, the lack of hair on top could be forgiven.

The mayor was the only elected official here—the Citizens Committee, which served as Hardy's town council, was appointed by him.

Seated next to Harris was a solidly built man in his distinguished forties, wearing a dark frock coat with a low-cut vest, light tan trousers, and a small bow tie sporting the pointed ends so fashionable in bigger cities. His hair was short and slicked down; his beard neatly trimmed; his nose hawkish; his wide-set eyes a dark, alert blue.

Willa had not met this individual, but she knew very well who he was. She also knew that the man's presence itself was offensive to her father, who was breathing hard, like a dog getting ready to bark.

Familiar footsteps in back of her, with an equally familiar jangle of spurs, told her a latecomer had made the meeting. She glanced just barely behind her at Caleb York, who took a position between the stove and the arrangement of chairs, standing with his hat in hand hanging loose at his side. He caught her eyes, nodded to her, and she flushed and turned away.

Willa and the sheriff had once been, as the gossips put it, an item. That state of things had shifted when York announced his plans to leave Trinidad for a Pinkerton job in San Diego, knowing good and well that she was not about to follow him—the Bar-O and her father were Willa Cullen's world.

That unhappy situation had turned to something tragic when she became engaged to a man York later killed.

Killed in the line of duty, for good cause, but when a former beau shot dead a current fiancé, the aftermath was bound to be awkward.

Mayor Hardy banged the gavel a few times and in his reedy tenor said, "Meeting will come to order. Our sole business today is to welcome and grant an audience to Mr. Grover Prescott. . . ." The barber's small mouth smiled under the big mustache as he nodded toward their hawkish-faced guest. "Of the Santa Fe Railroad."

Chair feet scraped the floor as those in attendance shifted and settled.

Hardy continued. "Mr. Prescott has come all the way from Albuquerque to speak to us about what he calls a singular opportunity for our God-fearing community— an opportunity that could bring prosperity and change to our little corner of the world. . . . Mr. Prescott?"

Greeted by cautious applause, the railroad man stood and came down around to the area between the audience and the Citizens Committee, the same space where lawyers for the defense and prosecution would plead their cases. Like one of those lawyers, he would prowl the area and make eye contact with the members of this jury.

Of course, making eye contact with Willa's father was out of the question.

"I guess I don't have to tell you good people," Prescott said, his voice deep and politician smooth, "that Las Vegas, your neighbor here in New Mexico, has gone from a bump in the road to a booming community rivaling Tucson, El Paso, and even Denver. They have gas- and waterworks, a telephone company, and six trains that stop daily! Your once-modest neighbor is in the midst of an unprecedented era of prosperity, dozens of new businesses springing up and flourishing, now that the Santa

Fe has transformed Las Vegas into a cattle railhead. It's fair to say that Las Vegas, like no other New Mexico town, has changed dramatically in the past few years, and for the better."

"Not entirely for the better," a male voice behind her said. That familiar, mid-range, mellow voice that seemed so unconcerned about anything at all.

Prescott, his rhythm thrown, turned toward the tall man standing at the rear of the seated group.

"Sir," the railroad agent said, a surface friendliness not entirely hiding his irritation, "I will be happy to answer questions . . . *after* I've completed my presentation."

"Well, I don't have a question, sir. It's more a comment."

All eyes were on York now. And Prescott had surely noticed the silver badge on the man's gray shirt, half covered by his black coat.

Prescott, cornered, said, "Well, go ahead, Sheriff. You *are* the sheriff, I take it?"

"I am."

"Well, be my guest. Speak."

If anyone was expecting York to come around and join Prescott up front, they were disappointed. He maintained his position at the rear, his head cocked at a lazy angle.

"Those new businesses in Las Vegas that have cropped up," York said, "include dozens of saloons and gambling halls and houses of ill repute. Murderers, thieves, shootists, swindlers, soiled doves, and tramps have all helped swell that population you mentioned. And their tourist trade has included in recent years, I believe, such luminaries as Doc Holliday, Jesse James, and Billy the Kid."

Prescott's frown stopped just short of a scowl. He paced as he spoke, but his eyes remained on York. "Tell me, Sheriff, are you against change? You surely realize that *any* booming community experiences growing pains. There will be churches and schools and flourishing businesses, and yes, the occasional desperado and dance-hall girl. But isn't that a small price to pay?"

Caleb's sly, shy smile was one Willa knew well. "Mr. Prescott, I am neither for what you propose nor against it. You haven't really proposed anything yet. I just want to make sure, when you do, that my friends don't buy a pig in a poke."

Mayor Hardy cleared his throat and said, "Sheriff, we appreciate you sharing your astute point of view. But perhaps we can learn from the mistakes of our neighboring community, particularly with a seasoned lawman like yourself to guide the way."

Caleb grinned and said, "Not for my current pay you can't."

That raised some laughter and even got a smile out of Prescott—a forced one, but a smile.

"Thank you for your insights, Sheriff," Prescott said with a dismissive nod. Then he turned toward the city fathers at their elevated table.

"Mr. Harris," Prescott said to their host, with a gesture around the room, "this is a fine establishment you have here. But are you aware that Las Vegas has become the territory's most important mercantile center? That since the railroad came in, over a million dollars in wool, hides, and pelts have been shipped out of there?"

Now Prescott turned to the town barber.

"Mayor Hardy, what is the population of Trinidad? Perhaps three hundred hardworking souls? Las Vegas is over twenty-five hundred in population now. You are at a crossroads, sir. Your fine little community can grow and thrive or risk becoming just another ghost town in the Southwest when times change and leave you behind."

Again, the railroad agent turned to address his audience.

"How can you enjoy the prosperity that has made a mecca of your neighbor? Very simple, my friends."

Prescott waved a slow hand across the air, tracing an invisible pathway.

He said, "The Santa Fe Railway intends to build a spur between Trinidad and Las Vegas, a branchline that will transform your community into a vital part of the cattle trade. But that is just the beginning. Your town will expand with new money, new blood, and fresh opportunities. We ask for your blessing, and your cooperation."

George Cullen stood.

The milky eyes trained themselves on the source of the voice that promised so much. The white-bearded chin came up, and a firm, determined voice came out.

"Mr. Prescott, you paint a pretty picture," Willa's papa said. "And you present this great opportunity to the citizens of Trinidad as if it's up to them to make this happen. But you and I know the truth, sir."

"Mr. Cullen," the railroad man said quietly, just a little defensive, "the Santa Fe does not go into a community blindly."

A murmur went up around them at this gaffe, and Prescott immediately understood his slipup.

"What I mean to say, sir," Prescott said quickly, "is that my company's policy is to inform a locality of our intentions, to seek their counsel and their support."

"I am happy," the old man said, sounding not at all happy, "to offer my counsel, but not my support. You are well aware, sir, that I control the vast majority of the cattle range in these parts. And I have no intention of granting you passage."

And her papa sat.

"Mr. Cullen," Prescott said through a strained smile, "with your cattle holdings, you will benefit as much as anyone—*more* than anyone—by having a railhead in your backyard. In addition, during the construction of the spur, we will need beef. I am more than happy, sir, to make arrangements with you to have our men fed. And, of course, the Santa Fe will pay generously for the right of passage. That remains for private negotiation, naturally, but do know that we are prepared to pay handsomely for these rights."

Without rising, Papa said, "If I was to do business with you and the Santa Fe Ring, *I* am the one who would pay 'handsomely.' "

The Santa Fe Ring her father referred to was a powerful cabal of attorneys and land speculators, with ties to the railroad, who had made a fortune in New Mexico through political corruption and fraudulent land deals.

Papa was saying, "Not only would your branchline disrupt my range, it would make it easier for my competitors to the south, from Texas to Mexico, to compete with the Bar-O."

"Sir—"

"*No*, sir. Right now the Bar-O has a short, two-day cattle drive to Las Vegas, and that gives us a market advantage that I have no intention of giving up. My fellow ranchers here should keep that in mind. At any rate, I'm quite satisfied to have things stay as they are."

Her father stood forcefully, and Willa rose, as well, then took his arm and guided him down the aisle between chairs, though truth be told, he was the one creating the forward motion.

She had seen him through the store and outside, down

to where the buckboard waited, and had even helped him up into his seat when she noticed Caleb York had followed. He stood on the boardwalk, in the blue shadow of its overhang, at the edge of the steps down to the street, hat still in his hand.

Why exactly she went to him, she couldn't say. He hadn't called out to her or even motioned, but she knew that he wanted a word.

She came over to the foot of the steps and looked up at him. Tall as he was, he fairly loomed over her.

Quietly, almost whispering, he said, "Is the old boy all right?"

Her father, up on the buckboard, was visibly trembling.

Sotto voce, she said, "He's fine. He's just mad, that's all."

"I don't blame him."

She glanced over her shoulder at her father and then back up at York with a frustrated frown, speaking softly. "Caleb, the thing is . . . I'm not sure I agree with Papa. I haven't spoken a word about it to him as yet, because I know how much it riles him . . . but he may be wrong about this."

"That so?"

She shook her head, and a yellow tendril came loose and dangled over an eye. "The railroad's the future, Caleb. There's no escaping it, and . . . and I'm not sure we should if we could. The branchline really will be a boon to Trinidad."

"Future's hard to avoid," York admitted. "And towns like this one either grow or fade."

Her frown turned confused. "I thought you didn't much care for what that railroad man was peddling."

He shrugged. "I just don't like being sold a bill of goods. There's generally two sides to things, and it's best to consider both. Anyway, there's a whiff of snake oil about that big bug Prescott."

She nodded.

Then an awkwardness settled in.

"Well," she said. "I should be getting back to the Bar-O."

"Well," he said. "Suppose you should." He smiled a little, gave her a respectful nod, and headed back inside.

For a moment there, it had been as if they were on speaking terms.

For a moment.

She got up on the buckboard and drove her father out of town.

When Caleb York returned to the meeting at the rear of Harris Mercantile, the discussion had broken up into groups of three and four. One such group included the Santa Fe man and three of the small-ranch owners. Perhaps Prescott figured he might be able to assemble a passageway through those lesser spreads.

York doubted that was a possibility. Cullen land had grown to include what had been the Gauge properties, when Willa's late fiancé had left his holdings to her. The other ranches formed a patchwork quilt that only rarely intersected and represented a small proportion of range at that.

The only straight shot at a pathway to Las Vegas from this part of the world was through the Bar-O.

Mayor Hardy was speaking with his fellow Citizens Committee members in the farthest corner, clumped together like the conspirators they were. The mayor noticed that York had returned, and waved him over.

York complied.

"Sheriff," the mayor said, "I hope your comments today don't find us at odds. Because the Citizens Committee is very much in favor of the Santa Fe spur."

"I can't say I've formed an opinion," York admitted.

"Then why did you make those comments?"

York shrugged. "It just seemed like Mr. Prescott was stacking the deck a mite."

Mercantile man Harris, eyes glittering, said, "Prescott isn't exaggerating when he says that branchline will mean great things for Trinidad—thriving economy, growing population. . . ."

"That doesn't sound like your words, Newt." York grinned at his host. "Or is there an echo in here from when Prescott was talking?"

Seeming to change the subject, Davis, the druggist, said, "Tell me, Sheriff, are you still considering that position with the Pinkertons in San Diego?"

"I assured you gents I'd stay at least till the end of the year," York reminded them.

"That's less than two months!" Mathers blurted, his muttonchops fairly bristling.

"We just thought," the mayor said with a nervous smile, "that you might stop to consider what this spur would mean to you . . . personally."

York grinned again. "You mean, I wouldn't have to wear my horse out whenever takin' a trip to Las Vegas?"

His Honor seemed about to put a hand on York's shoulder, then reconsidered it.

"What I mean is," Hardy said, "if that branchline comes through, we could offer you a healthy raise . . . a raise up to the level of what Pinkerton promises, and more. All kinds of perquisites commensurate with what that office would be. How would you like to live in a *house*, not a hotel room? A house the *city* would provide!"

Already they were thinking of themselves as a city, not a town.

York said, "That all sounds just fine. Would you throw in a housekeeper?"

"We could do that!" Mathers said.

But the mayor could tell York was having some fun with them.

"We're quite serious about this, Caleb," Hardy said. "Think of your fees for tax collecting in a city *ten times* our size. You'd have regular office hours, with a staff of deputies, and not just some old stable bum . . . meaning no disrespect to Mr. Tulley."

"Obviously not. But aren't you fellas forgetting one small detail here?"

The four men traded looks that said, *Are we?*

York opened a hand. "The most efficient and maybe only way that spur goes in is if George Cullen sells the right-of-way. Perhaps you missed it, but I didn't think he seemed all that enthusiastic about the prospect."

The mayor smiled so broadly that his handlebar mustache seemed to smile its own self. "That's where *you* come in, Sheriff."

"Do I?"

Harris took York by the arm. "Old Man Cullen likes you, Sheriff, respects you. You got rid of that evil bastard Harry Gauge, saved the old man and his daughter's lives out to the way station last year. That carries weight!"

Mathers said, "He'll listen to *you*, Sheriff."

York sighed, nodded. "He might."

The mayor said, "We need you to intercede for us with that hardheaded old fool."

That got a frown out of York. "George Cullen is no fool."

Hardy realized he'd misspoken. "Of course he isn't. But he's one of these self-made pioneer types who came to this country and carved out a place for himself. He sees the rest of us as newcomers, interlopers, and doesn't understand that times are changing and civilization is coming."

Giving York a patronizing smile, Davis said, "A man who's thinking about moving to San Diego and taking a job with the Pinkertons isn't a man who fears change. Isn't a man who ducks the future."

The mayor said, "Just *talk* to him. *Reason* with him. That is, assuming you agree with us and consider the branchline the path to the future for our little town."

So it was a town again. City would come later.

"I'll have a talk with Mr. Cullen," York said, gave the men a nod, and turned to go before he had to endure their self-satisfied grins.

On York's way out, Oscar Penniman, the newspaper-man, stepped in his path. York considered sweeping by and knocking him down in the process, then reconsidered. Probably best to maintain good relations with the press.

"Trouble you for a quote, Sheriff?" The editor's voice was casual, but his eyes were sharp, and the notebook was in hand, pencil poised. "My readers would, I'm sure, find your views on this subject of most interest."

"Not today, Mr. Penniman."

York slipped past the man, who tagged after.

"At the meeting you sounded skeptical of what might come of a branchline coming to town. Can I assume you'll take a stand against the railroad?"

"No."

"Then you're for it?"

"No, you can't assume anything. Quote what I said in there, if you like. Now excuse me."

They were outside now.

"*Sheriff!*"

The newspaperman's footfalls clattered along the boardwalk as he tried to keep up with the lawman's greater stride.

"Could you give me a quote on how you came to save that young man's life yesterday? You could have easily shot down that callow youth."

York stopped and turned, and the little man almost ran into him.

"He could have easily shot me," York said. "That's how gunfights work. *And* why they should be avoided."

The editor was scribbling in his notebook now, allowing the sheriff to make his getaway.

What York might have said was how he hated the idea of civilization squeezing all the life out of the Southwest. But why bother having any opinion on that subject? Change was coming. And a man might as well learn to live with it. Even a man like George Cullen.

Even a man like Caleb York.

CHAPTER THREE

The sun was well along on its western descent behind the Sangre de Cristo Mountains when Willa Cullen and her father rolled in under the rustic log arch with its chain-hung Bar-O plaque—a straight line above the *B*, imitating the Cullen brand.

Though their acreage had almost doubled in size, thanks to the Gauge holdings, which were now theirs, nothing about the ranch itself had changed a jot—corrals left and right, two barns, rat-proof grain crib, log bunkhouse, cookhouse with hand pump. The ranch building itself was mostly logs with some stone add-ons, the central wooden structure having been built by her father in the early days. Right now the cowpokes were still out with the beeves, the only sign of life a corkscrew of smoke emanating from the cookhouse chimney.

She brought the buckboard to a stop in front of the house, where her calico, Daisy, was tied at the hitch rail out front. Lou Morgan, the lanky old wrangler who looked after the barns, ambled up, spitting tobacco, as she was helping her father down. The crusty stockman took charge of the rig and began driving it over to the barn, where he'd unhitch the horses and guide them to their stalls.

Papa almost bounded up the steps he knew so well, propelled perhaps by his anger at the Santa Fe Railroad. She stopped to give Daisy a nuzzle, then went up the broad wooden steps to the plank porch to join Papa. That was when she noticed they had company.

Rising almost endlessly from one of the rough-wood chairs that graced the porch came a tall, sturdy-looking stranger who was perhaps fifty, with an easygoing smile that seemed to claim the right to do so. He wore a blue shirt and a brown vest with a red bandana at his neck; a dark brown Boss of the Plains hat was in his hand. He wore Levi's, and no gun rode his hip.

The clothes looked new, but their guest seemed weathered. That friendly face was oblong, trimly salt-and-pepper bearded, and the eyes in it were a dark blue that caught the light and reflected it.

"Don't you recognize me, you old reprobate?" their guest asked Papa in a voice both casual and rough edged. "Have I changed so doggone much?"

Her father froze at the front door, then wheeled toward the visitor, who was sauntering over to him with a jangle of spurs.

"Burt?" Papa said, his voice hushed, his eyebrows high. Then he said, "*Burt!*"

And lunged forward to thrust out a hand for the visitor to find, which he did, grasping it, shaking it. The man's friendly expression vanished, and sadness took its place, as the blindness of his host became clear by way of those milky eyes.

"George," the man said softly, "I hadn't heard of your . . ."

"My affliction?" her father said, grinning, their hands still clasped. "Seems age finally caught up with me. Anyway, I seen enough in my lifetime to last me two. And leastways I don't have to see what's become of you."

The easy grin broadened. "You'll just have to believe me, old friend, when I say I still cut a mighty strikin' figure."

They shared laughter.

The man called Burt turned toward her, releasing Papa's hand.

"You must be what become of that ornery tyke Willa," he said and shook his head and made a "tch" in a cheek. "Now look at you, so much like your mother."

"I'm Willa," she admitted. Suddenly her plaid shirt and jeans didn't seem feminine enough.

The visitor approached her and rather shyly said, "I'm Burt O'Malley. You wouldn't remember me—you were just a slip of a thing when I, uh, left. But maybe your daddy mentioned me."

She was lying, but it seemed right to say, "Oh, of course I remember you, Mr. O'Malley. And Papa has spoken of you often, and so fondly."

The latter, at least, was true enough.

The visitor raised an almost benedictory palm. "There'll be none of that 'Mr. O'Malley' nonsense. I'll accept Burt or Uncle Burt, and general terms of endearment . . . but no 'mister.' "

She took both of his hands in hers. "Uncle Burt it is. How did you get out here? I don't see a horse."

"I came by stage this morning to Trinidad and hired a man at the livery to drive me out in his buckboard. I'm afraid I've taken some liberties. . . ."

He gestured over to where he'd been sitting—next to the wooden chair was a carpetbag.

THE BLOODY SPUR 29

O'Malley said, "I kind of assumed I'd have a place to stay out at the Bar-O, least till I got my feet under me."

Papa was next to their guest now and slung an arm around the taller man's shoulder. "Today, tomorrow, and always, you're welcome here. Ain't you the O in Bar-O?"

She opened the cut-glass and carved-wood front door for them, and Papa gently nudged his old friend to go in first. Both men hung their hats on the wall pegs just inside to the right, then the sightless host led his friend into the sprawling central area of the house.

Like that fancy front door from Mexico, the living room retained her mother's touch, finely carved Spanish-style furniture mingling with her father's hand-hewn, bark-and-all carpentry. This was more her papa's domain than the late Kate Cullen's, however, with its beam ceilings, hides on the floor, and mounted antler heads. A formidable stone fireplace seemed protected by a Sharps rifle at left and a Winchester at right, each supported by mounted upturned deer hooves.

Papa had come west with that Sharps, and buffalo hunting had provided the funds that built this ranch. The Winchester was the tool of the spread's early days.

But George Cullen had not been alone in building the Bar-O. There had been Raymond Parker, who a decade and a half ago had sold out his share and was now a successful businessman in Denver. And there had been Burt O'Malley, as well, almost a legendary figure around here. . . .

Willa played hostess and made tea for the two men, who soon were sitting, sipping at china cups, in the twin rough-wood chairs with Indian blankets serving as cushions. She got a fire going in the fireplace they were facing.

Then, as she often did when inserting herself into the affairs of the men who dropped by to speak with her daddy, Willa perched on the stone lip of the hearth, positioned between the two men, with views of both.

They were reminiscing about buffalo-hunting days—that was when and where Papa, Parker, and O'Malley had met—when a lull came along, and she filled it, telling their guest that she had beef stew on the stove and that there was plenty enough for him.

"Very kind," O'Malley told her, "but the kitchen smells waftin' in done give you away. I'm happy to sit at your table, and I'm hopin' you Cullens can put up with me for a day or two, till I can line up lodgings in town."

"Nonsense," her father said. "We've a guest bedroom that is yours as long as you want it."

Sitting forward, Willa said, "And don't be embarrassed about asking for a helping hand. I'm sure Papa will stake you to—"

But Papa raised a palm, like an Indian chief in greeting, only what he meant was, *Silence.*

"Daughter, there's something I've kept from you," Papa said. "It was wrong of me, particularly since you have grown into such a strong young woman and, I am embarrassed to say, the real rancher on this spread. But you were just a slip of a thing when I made this decision, and I assure you your mother approved."

Willa leaned forward even farther, her brow creased with confusion. "Papa, whatever are you talking about?"

O'Malley was frowning, and he, too, sat forward. "George, are you saying your daughter has no idea what you've been doin' for me all these years?"

Papa sighed deep and, as he exhaled, nodded. "I'm afraid so. So much time passed, and it was just a . . . well, kind of a routine business matter, in a way."

"Papa!" Willa blurted, and if she'd leaned forward any more, she'd have been a pile of herself on the floor. "What in blazes are you *talking* about?"

Papa sat there, squinting at nothing, and licked his lips, mouth moving as if words were forming that refused to come out.

Finally, O'Malley spoke, his eyes on her steadily. "Willa, you know that Raymond Parker sold out his interest in this spread to your father years ago. . . . He's invested in businesses all around the Southwest. Denver, Kansas City, Omaha . . . owns hotels and restaurants, and, well, he's a very successful individual."

"That's Mr. Parker," she said, returning their guest's gaze. "But there were *three* of you in the Bar-O. You, as my father says, are the O, Mr. O'Malley . . . Uncle Burt. But my understanding is that you . . . you killed a man and went to prison for it. Or do I misspeak?"

O'Malley shook his head gravely. "No, you are quite correct, young lady. I indeed shot and killed a man. But it wasn't murder. Not in my view. They called it manslaughter, but in my mind, it was self-defense and somewhat of an accident. I can tell you about it, if you wish."

Sitting back, she shook her head. "Not my business."

He went on, anyway. Flames flickered reflectively on his lightly bearded face, and something distant came into his eyes and his voice.

"There was a woman we both loved. Or at least he *thought* he loved her—to me, it was something else. Something . . . base. Something animal. He was a rich man's son and a far better catch than me, in some ways, anyhow. Still, she rejected his advances and chose me over all his money . . . and this creature expressed his disappointment by . . . by forcing himself on her."

"Please . . ."

The flames reflected like flowing tears over the stony face. "Her name was Lisette. Pretty name, don't you think? For a pretty girl. She hanged herself the night before we were to be wed."

Though the fire was at her back, a chill went through Willa. Again, she said, "Please . . ."

"I confronted this vile excuse for a human in a Trinidad saloon, the Victory, which you must know of. His name was Leon Packett. Such a man's name is not worth remembering, but when you kill a man, even a man such as this, it kind of . . . sticks. He was handsome enough, I suppose, to go along with that wealth, and I think he usually got what he wanted from women, one way or another."

O'Malley sat forward, and his eyes looked past her into the flames; an intensity had him, and his words built, as if he were witnessing right now the past events he was reporting.

"He was at the bar, and I called him out. He turned toward me quick, and I drew and *fired*. But . . . he didn't have a gun. I *thought* he did. But he did not. Will you think less of me, Willa, if I tell you, even so, I'm not sorry I did it? But if that was murder, it was an accidental one. Hence, manslaughter."

"Thirty-year sentence," Papa said, "and Burt served twenty. Harsh sentence, but the dead man's family had money, as was said. Slice it any way you like, Burt O'Malley has paid his debt."

Willa turned toward her sightless father. "Is this what you were hiding from me? The tragic circumstances of Mr. O'Malley's imprisonment?"

O'Malley did not, at the moment, correct her into calling him Uncle Burt.

"No," Papa said. "I never concealed from you that Burt here shot a man and went to prison. You knew that much, if not the particulars."

O'Malley, his mouth smiling but his eyes unblinking, said to her, "The Kansas State Pen at Lansing, to be exact. Had to send me out of state. We *still* don't have a prison in New Mexico territory. Mite backward of us, don't you think?"

The story of how O'Malley came to go to prison had been a confession of sorts. Now it was her father's turn.

"Daughter," he said, and this time he was the one on the edge of his rough-hewn chair, the milky eyes on her, "when my good friend here was convicted of that crime, he signed over this ranch to me. Said he could no longer add to the Bar-O's well-being. Though he asked nothing of me, I told him I would put twenty percent of all our profits away for him yearly. That money has been banked in Denver, under Raymond Parker's supervision, and has grown to a considerable sum. Enough for Burt to start over and, despite the years stolen from him, still enjoy a share of success in this lifetime."

Behind her, logs snapped and cracked with flames.

"That seems fair to me," Willa said after a moment. She shrugged. "I have no argument with . . . with Uncle Burt receiving his fair share. You needn't have kept that from me."

O'Malley, settling back in his chair, flipped a hand. "I understand why your father was circumspect about sharin' with you his generosity to me. Explaining to you why he was salting away a portion of his hard-earned money for a murderer wasting away in a prison cell . . . ? Well, it would take a mature young woman to make sense of that."

She nodded, realizing this was a compliment. "I might not have accepted this arrangement so readily in my teens. Certainly as a child, I'd have been bewildered. But I know something of the world now."

Her father frowned, perhaps wondering whether she was referring to her kidnapping by the late, corrupt sheriff, Harry Gauge, or whether she'd possibly been thinking of the death by gunfire of her fiancé by the new, not at all corrupt sheriff, Caleb York. That she and Caleb had once been courting only made for salt in the wound.

But Willa referred to neither event, though both had certainly played a role in her new, more unsentimental view of things.

"I trust," O'Malley said to her father, "I'm not overstepping when I say that my intention, or at least my *hope*, is to buy my way back into the Bar-O. To be your partner again, George."

Her father said nothing, but his furrowed brow spoke volumes, which O'Malley had no trouble hearing.

"Is there something wrong?" their guest asked, obviously confused. "Considering your . . . condition, old friend, I would think having me around to help run things might be a boon. Even a blessing."

Her father remained silent, though he was clearly searching for words.

"Or perhaps," O'Malley said, eyebrows climbing, "I might suggest another path, considering your . . ."

He stopped here, but the word *blindness* was in the air between them.

Then O'Malley went on. "All that money you saved for me, George, has built up into a substantial sum. Perhaps we could reverse things, where I buy you out . . . including an ongoing, and most handsome, percentage of my profits."

This line of talk had sat Willa up. *Sell the Bar-O?*

"I'm afraid, Burt," her father said gently through a strained smile, "that's in no way possible. Y'see, I signed the Bar-O over to my daughter a while back, and I doubt she would consider selling."

Their guest gave her a lopsided smile. "So it's *you* I should be doing business with."

"This is still my father's ranch," she said, "in every sense but on paper. And the Bar-O is much larger now. When my fiancé died, I inherited a number of small spreads, all of which touch upon the existing Bar-O property."

With half a smile, O'Malley said, "Sounds like I might not be able to afford buyin' the Bar-O at that."

"But," Willa said, raising a gentle forefinger, "we might be willing to offer you one of those smaller spreads and to work together as the friendliest of neighbors. How does that sound?"

Nodding, O'Malley said, "Like a reasonable alternative, Willa. Did you have a certain ranch in mind?"

"There are several possibilities. We can ride out and have a look at them tomorrow. You can take your pick as it suits your pocketbook."

That was fine with O'Malley.

Soon the little group repaired to the dining room and gathered at the heavy, decoratively carved dark-wood Spanish table with matching chairs that her late mother had bought across the border.

Willa played hostess, serving the beef stew and keeping coffee cups filled, while the men reminisced about the early days of the Bar-O, back when Ray Parker was still a roughneck, not a "duded-up Denverite," as O'Malley put it. The sounds outside of the cowhands getting back and tying up their horses outside the bunkhouse and lining up at the cookhouse provided a muffled backdrop to the meal.

She had served the men and herself some apple cobbler when a knock came to the door, soft but audible. Wordlessly, she rose to answer it.

On the porch was foreman Whit Murphy, a lanky, bow-legged, droopily mustached cowboy of medium build in dusty attire—knotted yellow neck bandana, work shirt, Levi's, and low-heeled boots. Seeing Willa, he removed his tan high-beamed Carlsbad hat and gave up a shy smile.

"Miz Cullen," he said, "if I ain't bargin' in on supper, might I have a word with your daddy?"

"Of course."

He nodded toward the horse barn. "Lou says you got company, so we could talk out here."

"Nonsense. Come on in. Have you eaten?"

He stepped inside, spurs jangling. "No, but Cookie's savin' me some barbecue beef. Are you *sure* I ain't in-trudin'?"

"I'm sure," she said and took him by the arm and guided him to the dining room, where O'Malley stood with a smile to greet the newcomer.

Willa said, "Burt O'Malley, Whit Murphy. Best ranch foreman you could hope to meet. Whit, Mr. O'Malley here is the O in Bar-O—used to be partners with Papa."

Whit nodded as the two men shook hands. "I heard you spoke of," he said to O'Malley, which struck Willa as about as ambiguous a greeting as she'd ever heard.

"Sit with us, Whit," Papa said.

The foreman did.

Willa cleared the dessert dishes as Whit reported in on the day's work: the bulls had been herded and placed in an isolated pasture for winter, and the calves born since the spring roundup had all been branded. She smiled to herself when Whit raised his voice so she could still hear him when she stepped into the kitchen—the foreman knew who the real boss around the Bar-O was these days.

Willa's father asked her to fetch the brandy, and the three men enjoyed a drink and a cigar while she tended to the dishes. She was just putting things away when another knock came to the door, as loud and sure of itself as Whit's had been tentative.

This time she found a taller man on the Bar-O doorstep, one as unsullied as Whit Murphy had been dusty, all in black but for his light gray shirt with its pearl buttons and the matching kerchief at his throat. The Colt .44 on his hip hung low, though its tie was loose for riding. Down at the hitching post, his dappled gray gelding was tied next to Daisy, the former shaking its black mane as if to attract the latter . . . as if that would do either of them any good.

The last time Caleb York had come around, months ago, had been to tell her he had shot and killed the man she was engaged to.

"I do apologize," he'd said, hat in hand, "but he drew down on me. Just a pocket revolver, but I could've died of it."

Only later did she hear that Caleb had killed her fiancé with a nasty little knife called a Smoky Mountain toothpick. Somehow that had added insult to injury.

Still, she had come to know that her fiancé indeed had earned his fate, that he was a dastard whose scheming might have intended her own death—though she still found that difficult to believe—and there were those who said Caleb York had done her a favor, even a service.

But when the ex-beau kills the current fiancé, things are bound to get a touch tense, and the two had spoken little since that day.

He removed his cavalry pinch hat and faced her with an embarrassed smile; he would have to be so damned handsome, all reddish-brown locks and high cheekbones and sky-blue eyes squinting out at her.

"Miss Cullen," he said with a nod. "Might I have a word with your father?"

She stood framed in the doorway. "Whatever's happened between us, Caleb York, you still have the right to call me Willa. In fact, it would annoy me greatly if you didn't."

"Annoying you is not my intention," he said, risking another smile. "Is this a bad time? I know your father was worked up some after that Citizens Committee meeting."

"You'll find him in a much better mood now," she said, stepping aside and gesturing for him to come in. "Ever hear of Burt O'Malley?"

He hung his hat next to several others, on a wall peg. "One of your father's original partners, I believe? The O in—"

"Bar-O, yes. Just got out of prison. Killed a man. Some men have to pay for that, you know."

Caleb, who wasn't having any, said, "Not when they wear badges and who they killed drew down on them."

He took her by the shoulders and straightened her around to face him. They were a few steps into the living room now but far away enough from the dining room to speak without being heard.

"That man was a damned scoundrel," he said, "and I'm done apologizing for ridding the world, and you, of him.

Now, if we're going to be enemies over it, say so, and I'll go back to 'Miss Cullen' and we will keep our distance."

She drew breath in through her nostrils and scowled up at him. Then the scowl dissolved and she touched his face gently, "You're forgiven, Caleb."

"I don't believe I require forgiving."

"Well, you are, anyway."

He swallowed thickly. "May I suggest something, Willa?"

"Suggest away."

"Let's start with friends and see how that goes."

She nodded. "Fine idea."

So in a very friendly way, she took him by the arm as she walked him to the dining room. If her daddy were sighted, she wasn't sure she'd have done that. But he wasn't.

At the big dining-room table, introductions were made, and Papa invited Caleb to take a seat, which he did, to the right of Whit, who sat next to Papa and just down and across from O'Malley.

Caleb was offered brandy, and he took it, and a cigar, which he declined. Wordlessly, Willa sat at the table, a few chairs down from the men. In most houses, a woman dared not join the men for such a session. This was not most houses, and Willa was not most women.

O'Malley had a lopsided smile going as he studied Caleb. "So you're the sheriff of Trinidad."

"I am for now."

"Why just for now?"

"I have a job offer I'm considering, with the Pinkertons in San Diego."

O'Malley whistled. "That *has* to pay better than a small-town badge."

"They pay me well, and they're trying to tempt me into staying."

"Will that work, Mr. York?"

"It's Caleb. May I call you Burt?"

"Wish you would. So, Caleb, will it? Work?"

"That may depend on our host."

Papa, at the head of the table, almost choked on a sip of brandy. "Why would it depend on me, Caleb?"

"Well, sir, the local muckety-mucks, such as they are, are dangling a handsome raise and all sorts of extras before me—house of my own, among other things."

Willa, her voice small but clear from her end of the table, asked, "On what conditions?"

"On the condition," Caleb said to her, not quite smiling, "that I talk your stubborn old man here into selling the Santa Fe Railroad that right of passage they so crave."

Papa's face reddened.

O'Malley said, "Heard something about that in town. A spur, a branchline, is it? To Las Vegas?"

Caleb nodded, then added for her blind papa's benefit, "That's right, Burt. The city fathers see it as the future . . . and I agree with them."

Astounded, Papa said, "Caleb! You *challenged* them at their meeting! Talked of outlaws and harlots—excuse me, my dear—and the riffraff that would follow!"

"When a bump in the road," Caleb said, "turns into a railhead, many such bad things come, sure. But so do many good things. Saloons, yes . . . but also churches. Brothels, too . . . and schools."

"Trinidad is not my concern," Papa said, waving it off. "My only lookout is the Bar-O. Far as I see it, that town's just a place to buy supplies and do banking. When I helped bring it into existence, it was for my own convenience.

What advantage is it to me, turnin' that 'bump in the road' into a railhead? A railhead that can serve my *competitors*."

"Maybe nothing," Caleb admitted. "But one way or the other, the railroad will find a way to build their branchline. Maybe they'll cobble together passage from the independent small ranches. Or possibly they'll take their branchline idea to Ellis or Roswell or maybe Clovis, and you'll *still* lose your market advantage. If it's coming, why not be a profitable part of it?"

Whit Murphy, sitting quietly and taking all of this in, said, "Sheriff, if it's the small spreads that give up that right of way, it'll be a higgedly-piggedly thing that the railroad won't much cotton to."

Caleb nodded. "You could be right, Whit."

"And iffen that spur goes in at Ellis or Roswell or somewhere's, it won't hurt the Bar-O none. So why get involved with the railroad, anyhow? Bunches of men building the thing and spookin' the herd, then trains rollin' through, rilin' 'em further."

Caleb shrugged. "If it's inevitable, and I think it is, why doesn't the Bar-O benefit from that? Sell beef to the railroad workers. Sell that strip of land for a whole lot of dollars to the Santa Fe."

Whit snorted. "Sounds to me like you just want that big raise and that house."

Caleb grinned. "Well, of course I do. Why wouldn't I?"

O'Malley, who'd been studying Caleb, said, "You might have to pay too high a price, Sheriff. A bigger town, a Las Vegas–size town? Might find yourself a target every day of the week. Oh, I heard about that boy whose hand you broke this morning in Trinidad. That was a nice stunt. But he may come back at you, and that'll be nothin' compared to the parade of gunnies that'll come lookin' to make themselves a reputation in a boomtown version of Trinidad."

Caleb's smile again was barely there. "I appreciate the concern, Burt. I guess you know how bad things can turn out in a gunfight."

O'Malley's smile in return was similarly faint. And neither man had a smile in his eyes.

"I do at that, Sheriff," O'Malley said. "By the way, you wouldn't have ridden out here just to check up on me, would you?"

And now Caleb's smile blossomed. "Not *just* to check up on you, Burt. You stayin' in town or . . . ?"

"I'm staying here at the Bar-O, with these here gracious Cullen folks, for a short while. But after that, I'll be stayin' on in this part of the world. Might be I'll go into the cattle business myself. Thinkin' about buyin' a spread."

"I didn't think being in prison paid all that well."

O'Malley grinned. "Let's just say I made some wise investments. And when I get a spread of my own, I won't be selling no right of way to the railroad. No, sir. I'm with George on this."

"Well," Caleb said, making a sigh out of it, rising, "I've said my piece. I told the Citizens Committee I'd give it a try, and I have. That's all you'll hear from me on the matter . . . Burt, Whit, George. Have a pleasant evening . . . and thanks for the brandy."

Willa took his arm again and walked him through the living room. Caleb plucked his hat from the wall peg, and she opened the door for him. He seemed a little surprised when she slipped out with him, then shut the door behind her, sharing the porch with him.

"Caleb," she said, "I appreciate what you tried to do."

He frowned at her. "How so?"

She was standing close to him. "I told you before. Daddy's wrong about this! That branchline would be a real boon to Trinidad, *and* to the Bar-O. If . . . if you don't meet the future, it'll come looking for you!"

"That's nicely put. But I don't want to cross your father. Like I said, I've said my piece."

She shook her head. "No, Caleb. Keep it up. I haven't started working on him yet, not wanting to upset him . . . but when I *do* start in, I'll need your help."

She got on her toes and kissed him on the mouth, taking him by surprise, but the kiss lingered enough for him to get over the shock of it and enjoy it some.

And when he rode off, wearing the silliest smile she'd ever seen on him, Willa Cullen knew she had an ally.

At least.

CHAPTER FOUR

Caleb York, after taking a late lunch alone at the hotel where he roomed, remained at his table by the window, reading this week's edition of the *Trinidad Enterprise* in some borrowed sunshine.

He had slept in, having played poker at the Victory till the wee hours. Anyway, mornings were quiet enough that his deputy could handle things—and knew where to find him to rouse him if need be.

Again, he wore what was becoming his lawman's all-in-black uniform, but for the light gray, pearl-buttoned shirt. His Colt .44, not strapped down, pointed its holstered nose at the parquet floor.

The Trinidad House Hotel, the town's only such establishment, was typical in that its rooms were merely serviceable, while its lobby and dining room promised much more.

Under a high ceiling with cut-glass chandeliers, York was surrounded by dark wood, fancy chairs, and linen tablecloths and was attended by a waiter in black livery, who kept the sheriff's coffee cup brimming. The lunch had been typically good—an oyster omelet, a specialty of the house morning, noon, or night—and he sat digesting it as he read the front-page story of his near gunfight with that boy yesterday.

He had to give editor Penniman credit for getting the details right and only mildly exaggerating the jeopardy of the incident. The newspaperman hadn't been a witness to the near shooting but had gathered accurate enough eye-witness accounts. While not relishing being badgered by the man, York knew Trinidad could do far worse than the *Enterprise*.

Every town could use a paper to record murders, street fights, dances, pack-trains, church affairs, and highway robberies—all the things that said civilization had come west.

"May I join you for a moment?"

York glanced to his right and—*speak of the devil!*—there stood Penniman himself.

"Please," York said, gesturing to the empty chair across from him at this table for two.

The editor sat, removing his derby and placing it beside him at the table. The waiter came and delivered a cup of coffee without being asked. Penniman sugared it, sipped, then smiled, eyes wide and glittering.

"Well?" he asked, nodding to the paper that York was folding and placing to one side.

"I'm no expert on the art of writing," York said, "but you know how to get things across, and what I read's factual as far as it goes."

"How far does it go?"

"Mite too far. You're trying to make a hero of me."

The editor shrugged. "Well, you are one. And you're a boon to this community."

"Like the spur?"

A smile flashed below the well-trimmed mustache. "The spur is just a possibility, Sheriff. You're a reality. Someone famous among us. You make newcomers like me in Trinidad feel safe and at the same time . . . proud."

York sipped coffee. "Why proud?"

The little man's shrug was big. "You could wear a badge most anywhere. Las Vegas would hire you in a finger snap. Abilene. Dodge City. Tombstone. Of course, Tombstone *did* have a little trouble with having famous lawmen on the job a while back . . . but you take my meaning."

York glanced out the window beside them. "I like it here. I might make too regular a target of myself in towns of that stripe."

Now the eyes, sharp and dark, narrowed. "That so? Rumor is you're thinking about going to the big city. San Diego, to be exact. Going back to detective work with the Pinks."

"Not a rumor." York sipped more coffee. "That's been a plan of mine that keeps gettin' derailed."

"It will *really* get 'derailed' when that branchline comes in." Penniman leaned forward. "I hear you've been offered a hefty raise and a rent-free house of your own if the spur comes to be. And, anyway, isn't a man like you a target anywhere you go?"

"I intend to outlive that."

The editor smiled now, surprised by the remark. "What, one shoot-out at a time?"

The waiter came to refill their cups, and York held up a hand. Penniman's was refreshed; then York and the newsman were alone again.

"Times are changing," York said. "The Wild West won't be so wild before long. Just a bunch of towns, some big, some small, some in between. Like anyplace in America.

But what happened in Tombstone with the Earps and the Clantons—people are already making it clear they won't put up with that."

Penniman wiggled a finger toward the sheriff's folded paper. "Did you see my editorial?"

"Hard to miss on the front page."

The newspaperman flashed a grin. "Right next to the story about Caleb York. And you're in the *editorial*, too. I quoted you accurately, did I not?"

York nodded. "So . . . you're in favor of the branch-line."

The editor's wide smile challenged the narrow face. "Why, does that surprise you? Sheriff, I worked for fifteen years on the *Rocky Mountain News*, salting my money away, making my wife and children put up with second best. Took that long to save up for a small printing press. But I was determined to have my own paper. And now I have one."

"So you do. And a whole new building to yourself, with living quarters above and so much room to expand. But how was it you chose Trinidad?"

Penniman frowned. "Well, uh . . . just looked around for a town that lacked a paper, and—"

"And you had a silent partner in the Santa Fe Railroad, who suggested it."

Penniman flushed. "I didn't say that."

"I didn't say I thought there was anything wrong in it. But keepin' it to yourself does seem . . . What's the legal phrase? A conflict of interest?"

Penniman straightened. "Don't go spreading falsehoods, Sheriff!"

"I won't if you won't," York said pleasantly.

A figure in the window caught the attention of both

men, as suddenly Deputy Jonathan Tulley, just beyond the glass, was right there in all his skinny, white-bearded, baggy-pants glory, waving his arms like he wanted the attention of the world, shotgun in one hand, as if leading an Indian war party.

"I believe I'm bein' paged," York told the editor, gave him a smile and a nod, then headed out, leaving the slightly flummoxed little newspaperman to finish his coffee alone.

York plucked his hat from the hook just inside the connecting door with the lobby and moved through to step out onto the boardwalk, where Tulley was working up a lather.

"Sheriff! You know who just rode into town, big as life and twice as ugly?"

"No."

"Alver Hollis! Hear me? *Alver Hollis*! The Preacherman hisself!"

York had never met Hollis but knew all too well of him. Hell, most people working on either side of a badge knew of Hollis, and plenty more besides. No warrants were out for the so-called Preacherman, though the supposed onetime reverend was said to be a hired gun, with a gift for making his murders look like fair fights.

Murders that were followed by Hollis kneeling over each corpse he created to send the departed off with a prayer.

"Okay, Tulley. Calm yourself. He causing trouble?"

"*No!* He just got here. He's riding with a couple of saddle tramps I never seen before."

"You're sure it's Hollis?"

"It's Hollis, all right! I watched him one time over at Ellis. He goaded two men into drawin' on him at the same time, and sent 'em both to their reward."

"Pray over 'em both, did he?"

"Though it took two bullets, one prayer sufficed for both."

"Where are the man of God and his ungodly companions now?"

The former desert rat pointed down the street. "Where d'you *think*? They headed into the Victory like they owned the place!"

York sighed. "Tulley, the Victory's a business, open to the public, glad to have the likes of Hollis and his friends stop by. Those three are probably just passin' through. No need for us to borrow trouble."

The deputy squinted at his boss, as if trying to bring him into focus. "How do you know they ain't in town to take on the great Caleb York?"

York shook his head slowly. "Everybody who rolls through Trinidad with a gun on his hip isn't necessarily here to make a reputation takin' on the 'great' yours truly."

"The Preacherman ain't 'everybody'!"

York put a hand on Tulley's bony shoulder.

"Now, here's what I want you to do, Deputy. Go on down to the Victory, stake a claim on a table off to one side, and throw down as many sarsaparillas as you can stomach."

Tulley had been on the wagon for some time—sobriety was a condition of his employment, drunkenness being a condition of getting fired.

"If Hollis and his friends ride out," York told his deputy, "come find me and say so. And we'll be happy they stopped by to spread around some money in our fair community."

Tulley squinted again, this time more like he wasn't sure he was hearing right. "And iffen they *don't* ride out?"

"Keep an eye on them. See if they seem to be up to anything besides gambling and drinking at the Victory. Firing off their weapons, roughing up fellow customers, beating on the ladies, and such."

The deputy gripped his shotgun in both hands. "And unload on 'em?"

"No, Tulley. Go out the back way and come find me."

"Whereabouts?"

"Either at the jail, workin' on tax matters, or here at the hotel. *Comprende?*"

"*Comprende.*"

"If they take their horses over to the livery stable and check into the hotel, let me know. That means they are in town for some reason or another."

"Up to no good!"

"Good chance of that," York admitted. "But, Tulley, you can't run around like an Apache on firewater every time some rough character comes rollin' into town. As an officer of the law, you have to keep a cool head and a steady hand."

Still squinting, but nodding now, Tulley started down the boardwalk toward the Victory.

York called out to him. "Tulley!"

The deputy whirled, ready for anything, though he did trip over his own feet somewhat. "Yessir, Sheriff?"

"Take that coach gun back to the office and leave it there. Your badge, too. You're going down to the Victory as a customer."

A grin formed in the bristly beard. "Undercover like?"

York nodded and was able not to smile. "Yes. You're my undercover agent on this one, Tulley."

Tulley gave him a cautious salute, then headed back toward their office, leaving Caleb York trying to decide whether to laugh or cry.

*   *   *

York spent the afternoon filling out territorial tax documents and inventorying the $1,542.50 he'd collected last week from ranchers and farmers in Trinidad's portion of San Miguel County. This he took from the jailhouse safe and walked over to the First Bank of Trinidad, now a holding of George Cullen's friend Raymond Parker of Denver—after the previous owner had nearly bankrupted the institution. He deducted his 10 percent and deposited the rest in the city treasury account.

By this time, the western sky was striped with the red and purple of another fine New Mexico sunset, and two circumstances were presenting themselves: his stomach was again begging for attention and Tulley had not yet made a return trip from the Victory.

The latter could mean his deputy had fallen off the wagon, for which York would have to blame himself for sending the old reprobate into the arms of temptation. Both that and the former could be addressed by a sojourn to the Victory.

York tied his gun down and headed there.

Pushing through the batwing doors, York found a very lively crowd for a weeknight at the town's only saloon. The clientele included menfolk of Trinidad, mostly merchants and clerks and those who cleaned up for them, and a good number of cowboys whose workdays this time of year were finished by late afternoon and who, unlike trail hands, drew regular pay.

The gambling hall that took up much of the big room was hopping, roulette, chuck-a-luck, wheel-of-fortune stations, faro, twenty-one, and poker. At the far end of the saloon, its gold brocade walls decorated with saddles, spurs, and steer horns, rose a small boxlike stage with a piano by a skimpy dance floor, where locals and cowboys approximated dancing with silk-and-satin saloon gals.

Between the casino and the little dance floor was another major draw of the Victory: free food at lunch and supper. Right now a long narrow table seemed to separate gambling from dancing. It was covered in linen to rival the hotel's dining room and arrayed with cold cuts, yellow cheese, rye bread, celery stalks, pretzels, peanuts, smoked herring, and dill pickles. Such salty fare would lead inevitably to a thirst that needed quenching. And customers were drifting over to get plates of the stuff with beer steins in hand.

He found an opening at the bar, exchanging nods and greetings with his constituency, and ordered a beer, which hadn't arrived yet when he heard a throaty purr of a female voice behind him.

"Don't tell me they're charging you to eat over at the hotel, Sheriff! A man of your standing shouldn't have to go to a saloon to get a free meal."

The beer came, and he sipped it, tossed the bartender a dime, then turned with a smile and asked, "How's business, Rita?"

Dark-haired Rita, her slender, full-breasted frame well served by an emerald satin gown, said, "Middle of the week? Not bad. Not shabby at all."

He never tired of looking at that heart-shaped face with its big brown eyes, turned-up nose, and lush, red-rouged lips. The young woman had inherited the Victory from her murdered sister, who had also been a beauty, though a hardened one. Rita still had life left in her, and ahead of her, with any luck.

Raising an eyebrow, she said, "You have your badge on, I see."

He often played poker here and left his badge behind.

"Maybe I just forgot to take it off," he said.

"Or maybe you're here on business."

She slipped her arm in his and walked him to a table for four and sat herself down beside him. Over by the wall, Tulley was sitting with a sarsaparilla, trying to get York's attention with the subtlety of a mule-train driver whipping his team.

"I think your friend wants you," Rita said with a mocking smile.

"I think that sugar juice has gone to his head." He gave his deputy a sharp look, and the old boy settled down, looking a little hurt.

"He's been here all afternoon," she said.

"Maybe he likes the free lunch."

"And the free supper?"

"Why not?"

"He's had so much of that sarsaparilla," she said, "he's worn a path out to the privy."

"As I recall, that was already a pretty well-worn path."

She set her elbows on the table and folded her lace-gloved hands and rested her chin on them. Judging by her wicked little smile, she might have been propositioning him. But what she said was, "He's been keeping an eye on Alver Hollis."

"Has he now?"

"Ever meet the Preacherman?"

"Can't say I have."

"First for me, as well. Never saw those other two, neither, but it's too soon."

"Causing any trouble?"

She shrugged her satin-encased shoulders. "They've been drinking and playing cards all day—more or less behaving themselves."

"More or less?"

"I had to step in when one of them, the one missing his two front teeth, tried to get Molly to go upstairs with him. He didn't understand the new policy."

Rita's late sister, Lola, had run the upstairs as a brothel. Now the dance-hall girls were strictly that, and the upstairs had been transformed into fairly lavish living quarters for the young woman who owned the place. Her girls lived in a rooming house now, two to a room. If they wanted to see a man they met at work, they were free to. They could even charge those men for their favors. But not on these premises, and not at the rooming house, where she paid their rent.

York's jaw clenched. "Did he get tough with you?"

She gave him half a smile. "No. He wanted to, but Hollis stepped in and shut it down. Apologized to me. Took off his hat to do it. Real gentleman, if not quite a preacher."

"Interesting."

"You make something of that?"

"Maybe he's turned over a new leaf. Maybe he's not the bad man his reputation says he is."

"You mean, the way your reputation is undeserved? How you never hurt a soul? Never pulled that gun, never—"

"That'll do."

She leaned back. Folded her arms over the generous bosom. Cocked her head. Narrowed her eyes. "How many men have you killed, Caleb York?"

"I don't exactly know. Lost count at some point."

"How *did* you get that bad reputation?"

"I never killed for money, no matter what they ever said about me. I never killed a man who didn't draw down on me first. . . ." He knew that wasn't quite true, and amended, "Or who didn't need killing so's somebody could be rescued, say."

Hub Wainwright, the head bartender, came over to personally deliver a mixed drink to Rita. He was a big, skimpily mustached man who did his own bouncing. He leaned down for a private word.

"Miz Filley," he said, "I'm keepin' an eye out. No trouble so far."

"Thank you, Hub."

"I'll wade right in, need be."

"I know you will, Hub. Thanks."

Hub went back to the bar, like a bear heading for its cave, but without hibernation in mind.

She sipped the drink—a Sazerac. One of the fancy drinks that were popular because their rotgut base was so unpalatable. "So . . . you never saw the Preacherman?"

"No."

"Not even on a circular?"

York shook his head. "He's never been wanted for anything. He's careful about his kills."

With just a tiny toss of her head, Rita indicated the poker table over by the stairs. "That's him in the middle there, facing us. And on either side of him are his disciples."

Moving his chair a little, York got a good view of the men, all of whom studied cards in hand. Two of the players were scruffy, like if you hit them with a carpet beater, dust clouds would rise; they sat on either side of the man York figured they'd ridden in with.

The wiry saddle tramp at left had the missing front teeth Rita had reported, a week's growth of beard, and pop eyes that gave him a demented look. He wore a frayed work shirt, canvas pants, and a bandana that hadn't been washed any more recently than he had.

Similarly garbed, the guy at right was stocky and rough bearded, with shaggy brown hair and a piggy look. His fingernails were black with dirt, though York couldn't imagine this character ever working hard enough to get them that way. Digging somebody's grave he robbed, maybe.

The man who had to be Alver Hollis was dressed in preacher black, not unlike York—a black suit and hat, white shirt with a loose ribbon-style bow tie. Of average size, Hollis had an oval face with hooded light blue eyes, a narrow hook nose, a well-trimmed black beard, and a somber expression.

York shifted his gaze back to the lovely saloon owner. "Doesn't seem to be a need to make my presence felt. They're not causing any ruckus that I can see."

"So you'd be all right with them staying around town for a few days?"

He frowned at her. "What makes you think they're not just passin' through?"

"I spoke to Yancy when they took a break about an hour ago to help themselves to our grub."

She meant Yancy Cole, the house dealer, who right now was tossing cards to the Preacherman and his two follow-ers, as well as to a cowboy and clerk. His back to York and Rita, Cole was a self-styled Southern gentleman right off a riverboat—white round-brimmed, black-banded hat, gray suit, ruffled shirt.

She leaned close. "They made inquiries about the big game Friday night. That same one you're signed up for."

The house was putting on a draw-poker tournament, with a one-hundred-dollar buy-in—three tables, six players to a table, and, eventually, only one winner, who would take home two thousand dollars. Entrants from as far away as Las Vegas and Clovis were on board. York indeed had put his name on the list of players, intending to leave his badge and gun behind.

Suddenly, he wasn't so sure about the latter.

"All three signed up for the game?" he asked her.

She nodded. "The one with the toothless grin is Lafe Trammel. The pudgy one is Wilbur Landrum. And Hollis signed in using his own name. Preacherman doesn't seem to be playin' any games in town except poker."

"Better have a chat with the fellas," York said as he rose easily from the table.

Rita, still seated, said, "Try not to shoot too many customers, will you?"

York ignored that and ambled over to the poker table. As he went, eyes from all around the room followed him. He positioned himself just behind Cole, who gave him a backward glance and a smile as he shuffled. The Preacherman and his mangy choirboys were frowning at the newcomer.

"I'll just take a moment of your time, gents," York said, "since you're between hands."

Staying seated, the rabble on either side of Hollis scooted their chairs back and glared up at the sheriff. The Preacherman, though, stayed calm, his sky-blue eyes blinking lazily, his big rough hands linked prayerfully before him on the green felt. Chips piled on either side of the folded hands said he was doing well tonight. The idiots riding with him had skimpy stacks.

York said conversationally, "I understand you fellas are in town for the big game Friday night."

"What of it?" Trammel demanded, his upper lip folded up over the row of yellow teeth missing their central pair.

Somewhat belatedly, porky Landrum blurted, "Yeah, what the hell business is it of *yours*?"

Hollis, however, said nothing. Something like the start of a smile was forming, however, in that dark, well-trimmed beard.

York said, "Well, I'm the sheriff, and it's my business to protect this community. Mr. Hollis here has a name associated with homicidal violence. You two fellas seem to be ridin' with him. So I'm gonna have to insist that after that game—sometime Saturday?—you three ride on."

Trammel jumped to his feet. He was taller than York, which was saying something, but skinny and narrow shouldered. His hand wasn't near his holstered weapon, worn low because of his long arms, but he came over slowly to face York, eyes bulging, nostrils flaring.

"You got a hell of a nerve," Trammel yelled in a thin, raspy voice, "roustin' us for no damn reason, York!"

So they knew who he was. No surprise.

Trammel said, "We ain't done nothin' but ride in peaceable and drop some money in this goddamn slop chute!"

The skinny cowpoke was standing close enough that York could smell the nasty bouquet of beer and cold cuts on the man's breath.

"We could start," York said, his tone friendly, "with our town ordinance against public profanity. But more pertinent is, if you cannot show gainful employment or cannot show that you have some particular legal purpose to be in our town . . . you have to move on."

Trammel took a swing at York, who ducked under it and swung back, burying his left fist in his attacker's belly, doubling him over. York put his right fist so hard into the pop-eyed fool's face that its features seemed to collapse. Trammel backpedaled, blinking, trying to keep his balance, then bumped into the staircase post behind him, which startled him and sent him forward reflexively and right into another right hand courtesy of Caleb York. The taller man went down like a pile of kindling, and every bit as conscious.

The cowboy and clerk who'd been sharing the table with the Hollis party had disappeared like mist. The dealer was shuffling cards lazily, while the porky Landrum was on his feet, but not doing anything about anything. Meanwhile, the Preacherman sat, angled to take in the action, arms folded, his expression mildly amused.

Suddenly Tulley was there, scrambling around the fallen varmint, bending over to collect the man's gun, a .45, grinning up at his boss like the two of them had just defeated Santa Anna.

"*Hey!*" Landrum shouted at Tulley. "Give him his gun back! What are you doin' takin' that, you old fool!"

"This is my deputy," York said, "Jonathan Tulley. Tomorrow either he or I will be at our office, at the livery stable end of town, and Mr. Trammel can collect his weapon. He's lucky not to be spending the night in jail. Now sit down, Mr. Landrum, and maybe you can still play some cards, if your pal wakes up in the mood."

So far Hollis hadn't said anything.

But now York addressed him. "Mr. Hollis, as I said, you and your friends are welcome in Trinidad as entrants in the poker tournament. If you don't have business in town after, I will expect you to head somewhere that you do."

Hollis counted a handful of chips. Then, finally, he spoke, in a deep, resonant voice worthy of the circuit preacher he was said once to have been. "You hit my friend Lafe here so hard," he said, without apparent malice, "you might have knocked his front teeth out if somebody hadn't already beat you to it."

York glanced down to where the slumbering Trammel

was on his side, with a pool of bloody spittle on the wood floor beside his lips, a small yellow object, like a kernel of corn, floating in it

"I believe this time he may have lost one of his lowers," York said. "Mr. Hollis, you understand my terms? Welcome till Saturday morning, and then you face my displeasure."

"I do, sir. But might I add, 'Do not neglect to show hospitality to strangers.' Hebrews thirteen, two."

"'Woe to those who scheme iniquity,'" York said. "Somewhere in the Bible. Look it up."

He tipped his hat to the Preacherman, then sent Tulley off to the jailhouse to lock up the confiscated handgun, after which he headed over to the table of free food.

Despite Trammel's bad breath, York had built up an appetite.

CHAPTER FIVE

After supper, Willa and George Cullen—their house-guest, Burt O'Malley, riding alongside the buckboard on a borrowed horse—headed into Trinidad to pick up some supplies.

Normally, this kind of thing was done by sunlight, and, in fact, the sun was still around, though dying brilliantly over the mountains in a blaze of purple and orange. But Newt Harris of the Mercantile had asked her father to come in early evening and load up their considerable order of supplies so he might have a private word.

On the way, Papa grumbled about the imposition, complaining that this would likely be another attempt to make him see eye to eye with the rest of the Citizens Committee on the subject of the Las Vegas spur. She kept her opinions to herself, not yet letting the old man know she was, for once in her life, not on his side.

She did say, "Well, Mr. Harris has been a good friend for as long as I can remember. You owe him the courtesy of a listen, no matter what the subject."

Papa's nonverbal response was somewhere between a growl and a groan.

Normally, Willa—in a blue-and-black plaid shirt and jeans and work boots, hair back in a ponytail—would have been prepared to pitch in on the loading. But she was glad Uncle Burt had volunteered to come along, because she wanted to be at her papa's side when he and Mr. Harris spoke. She would not be excluded, because everyone in and around Trinidad knew that she ran the ranch as much as or more than her daddy these days.

Waiting on the boardwalk to one side of the entrance to Harris Mercantile were sacks of flour, sugar, beans, and rice, as well as small barrels of bacon packed inside bran, eggs packed in cornmeal, a tin of lard, a carton of Arbuckles' coffee, and a jug of molasses. Overseeing these was Lem, Harris's broad-shouldered, tow-haired, overalls-clad boy of twenty or so, whose greatest skill was fetching and carrying.

She parked the buckboard in front of the stairs up to the storefront and helped her father down. In his weather-beaten broad-brimmed tan hat, canvas jacket, gray flannel shirt, and Levi's, Papa might have been there to help load, as well; but this apparel, so much like what most of his hands wore—if a mite more expensive—reflected his attitude that he was just another working man at the Bar-O.

O'Malley hitched his horse, then came over to Willa, Boss of the Plains hat in hand. Just before father and daughter started up the steps, Uncle Burt gave her a look that said he'd handle things out here. She nodded at the big man, whose rumpled smile was a comforting thing, and took her father's arm and went up to the boardwalk, where Newt Harris was emerging from his store.

The heavyset, blond, mustached merchant was again in a medium-brown suit with a string tie, sending a message of serious business that would have clashed with her papa's attire, if he could have seen it. With a smile that tried a little too hard, Harris held open one of the twin doors to the store for them to enter.

They did.

Their host closed the door behind them. A single hanging kerosene lamp gave the store an eerie feel, not that the light during the day in here was anything but dim, either, the lack of side windows contributing to a dark interior. Long, merchandise-cluttered counters—candy jars, tobacco, stacked clothing—were on either side, and the walls were lined with shelves of household items and bins of foodstuffs. Hanging from the ceiling were coiled ropes, buggy whips, horse harnesses, and pails, throwing odd shadows.

In the midst of this looming commerce, which, of course, her father could not see, Harris and his two guests stood rather awkwardly. From outside came the creaks, whumps, and squeaks of sacked goods being hauled down and loaded up into the waiting buckboard.

Harris reached his hand out and found her father's and shook it a bit too eagerly; Papa released his grasp almost at once.

"I appreciate your business, George," the merchant said with forced cheer, "*and* your willingness to stop by for a chat."

"If this is about that goddamned spur," her father said, in a rare instance of taking the Lord's name in vain, "you are wastin' your breath, Newt Harris. We have contrary opinions, and let us leave it at that."

"George, please. Hear us out."

"*Us*? Why, is there more than one of you?"

From the rear of the store came figures forming out of

the darkness. It gave Willa a start, but she quickly felt foolish, realizing this was only the rest of the Citizens Committee—their barber/mayor Hardy, druggist Clem Davis, hardware-store owner Clarence Mathers, and undertaker Casper Perkins. The latter, a small bald man with a top hat for added height and a black frock coat for suitable dignity, hadn't been present at yesterday's more official and public meeting of the Citizens Committee. Perhaps he'd been busy with a client.

All the men, in a rehearsed manner that unnerved Willa almost as much as their appearance from the gloom, gave their names and said hello to her father, their fellow member. Each removed his hat as a symbol of respect, which, of course, Papa couldn't see.

Then, perhaps because the premises were his, Harris took the lead, even though the mayor was present.

"George," he said, his tone formal yet friendly, "we've gathered tonight to ask you, to *beg* you, to listen to reason. Trinidad needs the Santa Fe branchline. Needs it to grow. Needs it, frankly, not to die."

Papa said nothing.

Harris had run out of words already, so the mayor stepped in. "George, if Ellis or one of these other nearby communities gets the Las Vegas spur, our businesses will suffer and maybe wither away. We will indeed die. Trinidad will be just another ghost town."

Willa almost smiled at the word *ghost*, considering the strange angles and contours created on the faces of these businessmen thanks to that one hanging lantern. That the town undertaker was among them only added to the effect.

But her father, again, said nothing. His face, out of the kerosene-created shadows, was impassive, like something carved out of wood. Like the cigar-store Indian she'd once seen in a Denver hotel lobby.

The druggist spoke up. "You depend on my business when your cows and cowboys get sick, not to mention any family needs. George, if *I'm* out of business, think of the inconvenience to you! It's miles to the nearest apothecary!"

Papa said nothing.

The hardware man gave it a try. "You count on me for supplies, from screws to *clavos*, from hinges to gate handles. If Trinidad dries up and blows away, you'll be riding mile upon mile to fill them kind of needs!"

Papa said nothing.

She could hardly wait to hear what the undertaker had to offer, but he remained as silent as Papa. As silent as his customers.

Harris spoke again. "We hope to reason with you, George, to talk this out, talk it through . . . but so far you don't seem to want to give our side of it a fair look. If we can't appeal to your friendship, your sense of community, if not your own convenience, having a decent little town like Trinidad in your backyard, a town you helped establish, then maybe . . . just maybe . . . we can appeal to your pocketbook."

And from the darkness at the rear of the store came one last materializing ghost: a distinguished, wide-shouldered one in big city togs, with the eyes and beak of a hawk, and a beard barbered better than their mayor could ever have managed—Grover Prescott of the Santa Fe Railroad.

The Citizens Committee members parted like the Red Sea for their financial Moses, who stood facing their one solemn, stone-faced, obstinate member.

"Mr. Cullen," Prescott said in that politician's deep timbre, "my apologies for organizing this meeting and bringing you into it in a somewhat deceptive fashion. But my entreaties to meet with you at your ranch have met with no response. So I have leaned upon these good men of your community, your friends, your fellow committee members, to provide me with an opportunity to make you an offer."

Papa said nothing.

"Sir," Prescott continued, "I have spoken with the independent ranchers, who, with their smaller spreads, do not approach the acreage you yourself control. But together they could provide the Santa Fe with the necessary right-of-way. . . ." Prescott chuckled. "Granted, that passage will have rather more twists and turns than a branchline might ideally have."

Papa said nothing.

"And that is why, Mr. Cullen," Prescott said, undiscouraged, "we are prepared to pay you twice the collective sum we have offered those smaller ranchers."

Papa said nothing.

"Furthermore," Prescott said, ramping up his vocal delivery to where various objects in the storefront rattled and shook, "we would happily make a side arrangement with the Bar-O to purchase beef for our workers during the branchline's construction. In addition, we would pay rent for the tent city that will follow the workers on their necessary course."

Papa said nothing.

Prescott asked, "Would you like to know what that offer amounts to, sir? Or would you prefer to discuss it out of the earshot of others?"

Again, Papa said nothing.

But he did provide a response of sorts: he turned and headed out, with a confidence that a blind man ought not have, but his daughter was there to guide him when he slightly misjudged the door.

Outside, big Lem was loading up one last sack of flour, with O'Malley supervising, as Papa came down those steps with Willa on his arm, frightened her father might lose his step, driven by temper as he was, his face as red as the stubborn streaks of the dying sunlight.

Rattling down the stairs came their frustrated host, while the other committee members followed, pausing on various steps behind him. Grover Prescott was not among them—he'd disappeared like the ghost he'd first seemed to be.

Harris caught up with Papa and spun him around, shouting, spittle flying. "You muleheaded old fool! You're going to ruin it for the rest of us! Now, come back inside and talk this out reasonable like!"

If any blind man ever threw a better punch, history had not recorded it—at least not that his shocked, and rather proud, daughter knew of.

While she was for her own reasons in agreement with these town fathers, their attempt to manipulate and pressure Papa, and even, in the case of Prescott, buy him off, enraged her.

The old man's blow having landed right on the chin, Harris stumbled backward, only to get caught by Perkins, who had followed him down the steps.

And, of course, being in an undertaker's arms could only be disconcerting, so the merchant got his footing back and was starting to form words with a bloodied mouth when a hulking form came between him and his blind attacker.

Lem bashed Papa in the face a good one, and Papa went down hard.

Willa knelt at her startled father's fallen side and looked up at the lummox and snarled, "Get away from him, you blooming idiot!"

But the blooming idiot just stood there with his fists balled, looming over his sightless elderly opponent like he was ready to continue the fight, and he got his wish when big Burt O'Malley came out of somewhere to send a swift fist into the dolt's breadbasket and another into his face.

Lem stumbled back, even as his father and the other committee members were scrambling out of the way, some almost scampering back up the steps to the boardwalk, as if seeking a better viewing position.

Like his father, the big kid in overalls had a bloodied face; but he was as tough a nut as O'Malley, which meant the fight was on.

Lem came at his father's attacker fast, long arms windmilling, displaying no skill but plenty of power, forward movement that sent the older man backpedaling out into Main Street. Here a dust-reducing layer of sand from the nearby Purgatory River had been spread, which effectively slowed both men down. This was not good news for O'Malley, who might have benefited from fancy footwork and who, for all his size, was smaller than the younger man and now had to stay more or less in one place while trying to keep under those long, lashing arms with the rocklike fists on the ends of them. O'Malley did fine for a while, but finally one of those wild swings clipped him on the forehead and he went down on one knee.

Somebody must have taught Lem it wasn't fair to keep hitting a man when he was down. Maybe Mr. Harris, knowing his boy's power, had advised him of such in childhood to keep his son from killing somebody.

So Lem paused just long enough for O'Malley to scoop up a handful of sand and toss it in the big lug's face. This sent Lem stumbling back, blinking, brushing his eyes with fingers too busy to be fists right now, and O'Malley came forward with a flurry of punches that were anything but windmilling, that were directed with precision, kidney punches alternating with a barrage of belly blows.

Clearly, the older man knew more about fisticuffs, so somehow the dim boy got bright enough just to tackle his opponent, and they rolled and wrestled and got in blows here and there, some glancing, some damaging, and it might have gone on a good deal longer if the gunshot hadn't rung out.

All eyes, including the combatants', flew down the street to the Victory on its corner perch, where standing just outside the batwing doors was the sheriff, all in black, his .44 aimed skyward and gun smoke trailing in that same direction. Just behind him, looking on with concern, a hand on his shoulder, was the dance-hall queen, Rita Filley, looking so lovely in that green satin gown that Willa couldn't have hated her more.

"*That's enough!*" Caleb York yelled toward them.

Then he strode their way, spurs jingling, and the older man and the younger one got off each other, as ashamed as a girl and a boy caught in a hayloft with their clothes askew.

O'Malley was brushing sand off his clothes, while Lem just stood there bleeding, as Caleb came up, then holstered his weapon when he saw the battle was over, at least for now.

"Is this about anything?" the sheriff demanded.

Nobody said it was. Willa had long since helped her father up, though he still looked dazed, even for a blind man.

"Find someplace else to be," Caleb told them.

The merchants and the mayor all walked in their various directions, while O'Malley and Willa got her papa up into the buckboard.

Then she came over to Caleb and said, "Thanks for breaking that up."

"What they pay me for."

She gestured toward the committee members, who were fleeing toward their respective homes. "They were trying to pressure Papa into selling that right-of-way."

"I gathered."

Very quietly, after a glance back at her father, she whispered, "They're makin' it hard for me to agree with them."

He grunted a laugh. "I know the feeling. But people can go about something the wrong way and still be right."

He walked her to the buckboard, helped her up.

"You all right, sir?" Caleb asked, looking across Willa at her father.

The old man sat slump shouldered, as if he'd been defeated, even though she'd watched him spurn such heated attempts to make him knuckle under. All Caleb got out of her papa was a nod.

Then Caleb gave her a nod and said, "Willa."

She nodded back, reins in hand. "Caleb."

The sheriff touched his hat to O'Malley, already on horseback, and O'Malley did the same, wearing that easy smile. He didn't look much the worse for wear. Just a bruise forming on his forehead, where Lem had clipped him.

Caleb said, "I take it you waded in to help Mr. Cullen."

"Somethin' like that."

"Obliged."

"Glad to help out. Nice to know I can still handle a jackass kid if need be."

"Comes in handy," Caleb said, though, of course, it had taken the sheriff's gunshot to end the fight.

As they rolled out of town, with Willa at the reins and Uncle Burt riding alongside, she glanced back at Caleb, who was walking toward the Victory again.

Where Rita Filley waited on her doorstep.

CHAPTER SIX

Alver Hollis had never really been a preacher of any kind. His *father* had back in Ohio, and it was from that very real Baptist minister that Hollis had learned the Bible inside out, and been frequently beaten with the Good Book, as well. Also with various belts and a razor strop, as evidenced by the scars Hollis's flesh still bore.

Not that his righteous daddy had needed anything but the two massive fists God had given him. From his pulpit, Hollis's old man—a tall, broad-shouldered figure with blazing eyes in a black-and-white-bearded face— promised his flock fire and brimstone. He scared the hell into and out of them, but only his boy knew how much terror this man of God could deliver when words weren't his only weapon.

One afternoon, when his mother—God bless her—was away, seventeen-year-old Hollis had shot his father six times on various parts of his body. This included, stigmata-style, the palms of his upraised, begging hands, but not the man's head, because that crown of thorns would have seen the mean old bastard dying much too soon. How Hollis had relished the variety of expressions—surprise, pain, rage, fear, and various shades of each—that crossed his father's face as the man died there in his study, crumpled on the floor by his desk, a towering figure no more, surrounded by all those books about God and sin and salvation.

As he'd planned, Hollis had quickly packed a bag, mostly with his father's clothes, since all he had were a couple of shirts and pants and a pair of shoes. He'd taken the money from the tin box in the desk—seventy-five dollars, a fortune—his dead father on the floor making no protest, before saddling up the best of the buggy horses and making his way to the wagon train outside Springfield.

Wearing his father's black frock coat and hat, and sprinkling his speech with the many Bible verses he'd swallowed, if not digested, Hollis was assumed by one and all to be a godly man. Or at least that was the case before he was thrown off the wagon train somewhere in Colorado after two married women got into a fight over him and one of their husbands drew down on him, dying for it, of course.

By that time, he carried with him the nickname "Preacher," granted him by those around him before they understood his true nature. And as he rode through the West, perfecting the lethal proficiency with a six-gun that he'd first demonstrated back home in his father's den, Hollis would never correct those who assumed he was a real reverend. Or that he at least had once been one. And he was barely twenty before the "man" got added on to "Preacher."

The Preacherman fell into his self-created profession gradually. He had no desire or training or, for that matter, talent for any usual Western trade. Cowboying was too hard and too dirty, and prospecting was harder and dirtier. He was no damn clerk or farmer, turning his nose up at anything menial, and much of the outlaw life didn't appeal to Hollis, either. Rustling or claim jumping was, after all, just a left-handed way of cowboying and prospecting.

So what might he be good at?

First, he had a way with a gun—he was fast and accurate, a skill enlarged upon by his lack of respect for any human life but his own.

What else?

Well, from his father he had picked up a certain bearing, an unearned dignity that attracted others to him. Farmers had him over for Sunday dinner; politicians running for office invited him to sit up on the stage; merchants either charged him nothing or provided a discount. Churchgoing women invited him in when their men weren't around; trollops never asked to be paid; virgins sought his religious guidance, only to be schooled in sin.

More important than these disposable females were the gutter gunhands who gathered around him like flies to honey. He'd been through almost as many of these creatures as he had women. At first—discreetly, not wishing to spoil the false impression of piety he would ride into town with—Hollis had gathered such would-be desperados in the one line of outlawing he could stomach: robbery.

Starting out with stagecoaches, Hollis would ride at the rear of two or three masked others and shout orders. His boys would be in the line of fire, dealing with stagecoach drivers, shotgun guards, strongboxes, passengers and their possessions—and if somebody got brave, Hollis would not be the one who got the bullet. He lost four or five boys in this line of work, and the one bank he robbed saw two more buying it before Hollis got a bullet hole through a perfectly good black Stetson. Enough of that!

But by this time, he had a stake, and he took up traveling alone again and set upon gambling, which was another of his talents. At this point he was mistaken less and less for a godly man, the suggestion now being that he had once ridden circuit but had lost his calling, if not quite his faith. And it was as a cardsharp that he accidentally came upon his unique profession.

On three different occasions—*three*—he was accused (rightly, but that is incidental) of cheating at poker. On each occasion he taunted his accuser—with " 'The Lord detests lying lips,' Proverbs, twelve, twenty-two," among other appropriate shaming verses—goading them into drawing first.

With his speed and accuracy, Hollis had no problem besting these challengers. He wouldn't even bother getting to his feet before drawing his Colt Single Action Army .45 and sending them to glory. In no instance was he held longer than an hour before a local lawman or justice of the peace declared the killing self-defense. Only once in those three times was he asked to leave town.

The three dead men were a cowboy, a rival tinhorn, and a local rancher. The variety of the victims encouraged him that he might be on to something. His reputation as a gunfighter inevitably led to backroom offers by various respectable types, mostly wealthy but sometimes merely successful merchants seeking to remove some human obstruction from their path. While flat-out murdering somebody seemed risky to Hollis, and a little distasteful, killing someone in self-defense was both an interesting challenge and a legal way out.

That was how the Preacherman's profession developed. If you wanted a man dead, you crossed Hollis's palm with the requisite silver. And here was where the challenge came in, as the Bible verse–spouting hired gun would needle and insult the intended victim, sometimes over days or even weeks, until that victim pulled on him. In this manner, Hollis protected his client, since the grudge appeared to be between the victim and Hollis himself.

The two currently riding with the Preacherman were typical of the rabble he periodically gathered—lowlifes attracted by his killing reputation who would settle for crumbs from whatever bread he might bake.

This pair—Trammel and Landrum, a scarecrow and a porker—were no better or worse, no smarter or dumber than those who'd preceded them. Their function was to be there to back Hollis up if a victim turned out to have unexpected help. Friends of a sort to handle any real friends the target might have.

Right now, the Preacherman and his two-man congregation were seated at a wobbly table in a two-story adobe structure that might have been a church. They had walked up here from the Victory not long after the sheriff knocked Trammel down and took his gun away.

The Cantina de Toro Rojo was no house of worship, however, rather a temple of sin looming over the humble adobes huddled along the narrow lane that led here. Trinidad's modest barrio, its inhabitants like the slumbering serfs of a medieval castle, lay silent but for this lively cantina.

Hollis had been in dozens of such watering holes—straw covering the dirt floor; walls of yellow, their once bright murals now faded to pastel. A little hombre in a sombrero tickling a cheap guitar; a fat, sweaty bartender with a droopy bandido mustache, his bar a couple of planks on two barrels, with no stools. A scattering of mismatched tables and chairs, the ghost of refried beans haunting the place, no food service this time of night.

The all-male clientele ranged from gringos, both cowboys and town folk, to Mexicans, the latter vaqueros from area spreads, with a few black cowboys on hand, too. Nobody seemed to care. That included four young señoritas with old eyes who circulated open-mindedly. Lots of dark hair rode their bare shoulders; their peasant blouses threatened to spill their contents like fruit from a basket; and black skirts striped with red and yellow and green, plump with petticoats, swirled and twirled. They were not waitresses—you went to the bar yourself for that kind of service.

These soiled doves had rooms upstairs, where they lived and worked. Two others were already up there working, not living.

Hollis was having mescal; the other two, beer in warm bottles. Trammel was staring at a pleasantly plump strumpet who was working a table over by the washed-out mural of a bullfighter, a guitarist occupying a nearby corner. Laughing, she sat sideways on the lap of a black cowboy, facing him, arms around his neck, but also displaying her legs to other potential clients, in case this didn't work out.

Trammel's pop eyes were half closed, which was no one's idea of a pleasant sight, and his upper lip was curled back over the smile whose missing two front teeth made a window onto his throbbing tongue.

"That ain't right," the lanky saddle tramp began muttering. "That ain't right nohow, no way."

Hollis, who had relieved the bartender of the bottle, poured another shot of mescal. He had no interest in what Trammel was talking about.

But the pig-faced Landrum did. "*What* ain't right, Lafe?"

Trammel shook his head. "Piece of calico makin' eyes at a black bastard such as that, and him lappin' it up like cream. You *see* that, don't you, Wilbur?"

Landrum, who clearly hadn't given it a bit of thought, now frowned in outrage. "Oughta be a law. Oughta be a damn *law*!"

Both of the Preacherman's altar boys had been drunk before they got here, making any meaningful business conversation with them a "filling an inside straight" long shot. But he would try.

After savoring a smoky sip of mescal, Hollis said, "I met today with that old friend of yours, Lafe."

Trammel removed his awful eyes from the Mexican girl and the black cowboy and applied them to his boss. The gap-toothed frown became a grin. "How *is* the old buzzard? Does he get why I best not be seen with him?"

Hollis nodded. "He appears fine, but the question is, do *you* 'get' why you can't be seen with him?"

"Well . . . because you said I oughtn't."

"But . . . the reason?"

Trammel sucked air in through his grin. "Might start people to talkin' or such like."

"Good. Yes, it might. And I won't be meeting with him myself again until the job is done."

Trammel leaned forward in a conspiratorial manner that fairly shouted secrecy. "Did he say who he brung us here to do in?"

"He did. Did indeed."

Now Landrum sat forward, like a baby bird wanting its portion of worm. "Ain't you gonna fill us in, Preacherman?"

Hollis shook his head, his expression somber. "No. I think it best I keep to myself the object of our attentions until we're closer to the actual carrying out of the task."

Trammel frowned, not angry—more like hurt. "Don't you *trust* us, boss?"

Hollis raised a benedictory hand. "I trust you, but not your discretion. 'Let no corrupting talk come out of your mouths,' Ephesians four, twenty-nine."

His two helpers thought about that, as they often did when he quoted scripture.

Then Landrum said, "Well, I sure as hell hope we get to stay around town till after that poker match. Might be some easy pickin's."

Hollis, knowing Landrum was a miserable poker player, nonetheless nodded. "You'll have that opportunity. In the meantime, enjoy yourselves, my friends. This, by the way, is the only house of ill fame available in Trinidad."

Big eyes rolling, Trammel said, "I learned *that* the hard way. That woman what runs the Victory says her girls ain't harlots no more. What's the good of a dance hall in such case?"

Hollis took another smoky sip. "Civilization is coming to the West, my friends. No getting around it. We must adapt or go the way of the buffalo."

Forehead creased, Landrum said, "The buffalo got shot."

"Yes, and that's because they were dumb beasts. We are God's children, blessed with the gift of thought. Of reason. We will fit in as times change."

Trammel wasn't listening now. He was again frowning over at the Mexican girl and the black cowboy. They were four tables away and apparently hadn't noticed his gaze, though that particular gaze would seem hard not to notice.

But Landrum was interested in what his boss was saying. "If times is changing, how does gunfighters fit in?"

"Eventually," Hollis admitted, "they won't. Not as we know them. But guns aren't going anywhere. And there will always be people eager to hire their use. And other people ready, willing, and able to fill such requests. 'For from within, out of the heart of man, come evil thoughts,' Mark seven-twenty-one."

Trammel, this time ignoring the word of God, held his hand out to his porky compadre without looking at him. "Gimme your gun, Wilbur."

Landrum blinked at him. "What?"

"Your gun! Gimme your gun. That damn deputy at the Victory took mine!"

"What you want it for?"

Hollis sighed and put a hand on Trammel's arm. "There are plenty of choices here among the señoritas. Be content with one who does not already have a customer."

Trammel didn't appear to hear. He thrust his open palm more forcefully at his porcine companion. "Wilbur! Your goddamn *gun.*"

The gun was handed over, and Trammel stood, sliding the weapon—a nasty-looking Remington—into his low-riding holster. A decent fit.

"I implore you, my friend," Hollis said, "not to cause yourself, not to cause *us,* any needless trouble. 'The hot-headed do things they'll later regret,' Proverbs fourteen, seventeen."

But Trammel still didn't seem much in the mood for theological counsel.

He strode across the room, long arms swinging, just as the unwitting cowboy and the girl got to their feet and headed, smiling, arm in arm, for the door. They were apparently on their way to a room upstairs, accessed by an outside flight of stairs.

Trammel, spurs singing a discordant tune, stalked over and put himself between the couple and the exit.

"Some things just ain't right under the sight of God," Trammel said.

At that moment, Hollis—still seated with Landrum at their table—wished he hadn't filled Trammel's skull with so much scripture. He considered interceding and trying to stop what otherwise would be an inevitable tragedy, but putting himself in the middle of this might risk what they'd come to Trinidad to do.

Trammel would either survive or not. With a shrug, Hollis poured himself another glass of mescal.

The coffee-skinned cowboy wore a yellow bandana, a broad-brimmed felt hat, a blue cavalry jacket over a lighter blue shirt, and light gray "California"-style wool pants with loose-fitting legs. He was big and tall and as good looking as Trammel wasn't, the harlot hanging on to his arm like a bosomy appendage.

A Peacemaker rode his right hip, high.

The cowboy's voice had a low, rich timbre. "You have a problem, mister?"

"I got a problem called niggers putting their hands on their betters."

The harlot's eyes and nostrils flared. "I am *mexicano*, you crazy-eye fool!"

The cowboy knew what was coming and pushed the girl aside, and she went clattering into the table they'd just vacated.

But that gave Trammel all the time he needed to draw and fire, while his opponent's hand was barely over his holstered .45. The bullet punched its way through the cowboy's chest, blood and general gore splattering the bullfight mural.

Damned good shot for a drunken fool, Hollis thought.

The black vaquero teetered on his heels, taking a few seconds to come to terms with his own death, then fell back and landed hard on the straw-strewn floor. Chair legs scraped and señoritas screamed, the fat mustached man behind the bar shaking his head with disgust as he wiped a glass with a rag.

What the hell? the Preacherman thought. In a place like this in this part of town, a shooting wouldn't amount to much. Hollis was digging some half eagles out of his pocket when he saw something that, for the first time this evening, caused him alarm.

That bearded old coot of a deputy stood in the doorway, a double-barreled shotgun over his arm.

Jonathan Tulley, after locking up that sidewinder Trammel's .45 in the jailhouse safe, had not returned to the Victory, having had his fill of sarsaparilla for one night. Instead, he had taken up the nightly patrol, which was a big part of his job as deputy. This consisted of checking doors and alleys on Main Street, and walking the side and back streets to make sure no devilry was afoot.

When he collected his scattergun at the office, the wall clock had said 11:10 p.m. This was late for him to be starting patrol, which he usually began at sundown and kept up till the Victory was shut tight. But tonight was different: he'd had that special undercover assignment from the sheriff, to hang out at the saloon and keep an eye on the Preacherman and them two hard cases he rode with.

Often Tulley made the barrio, that shabby cluster of low-slung adobe-brick buildings opposite the jailhouse, the last stop of his night patrol. That was because the deputy lived at the office, sleeping on a cot in one of the cells. And saving the barrio for last left Tulley close to home when he finished up.

In his loose canvas trousers and BVD shirt, Tulley found the night cold enough to give him some shivers. The sheriff had advised him to spruce up his duds some, more suitable like to a deputy, but Tulley had never got around to it. He had a daughter in Denver, living with his brother and wife; he was saving up money for the girl. Ella would be sixteen now. Last saw her at six, when her mother died of the smallpox. Anyway, he liked that BVD feel, though a buckskin jacket this time of year might make a wise investment.

His shotgun over one arm, Tulley started down the central lane of the modest barrio, which was quiet and dark now, the dusty path free of barking dogs and scurrying chickens, not a light burning in a single window. That is, not a one till he approached the two-story structure at the dead end of the facing rows of adobe huts. There the windows glowed yellow on the first floor, with more yellow above, thanks to flickering candlelight in rooms where them fallen women practiced their sweet and sinful trade.

Big, red, weather-faded letters above the archway door said CANTINA DE TORO ROJO. A cowboy and a señorita sauntered out, hanging on to each other, both three sheets to the wind. They went up the exposed wooden staircase on the right side of the place, and Tulley saw the female wasn't as drunk as she pretended to be.

Horses lined the leather-glazed hitch rail; guitar music

and conversation murmured at the open windows. Nothing out of the ordinary. Tulley made his way to the door and was almost inside when the gunshot shook the room, and the deputy.

That same saddle bum who had given the sheriff trouble at the Victory was standing there with a big smoking six-gun in his hand, looming over a cowboy on his back on the floor, staring up with eyes that weren't seeing a damn thing. People were on their feet and would have rushed out if Tulley and his scattergun hadn't been in the way, and the señoritas were screaming their fool heads off—in particular, the one near the shooting.

"*Just hold 'er right there!*" Tulley yelled, and he swung his shotgun to and fro so's people could tell he was serious. The badge on his chest said the same.

That tall, skinny Trammel was looking over his shoulder at Tulley with them weird bulging eyes, and the deputy let him use them bulgers to have a look down the twin black holes of the shotgun.

"Set that iron down, sonny," Tulley said. "Slow and no tricks. You wouldn't look no worse with your head blowed off."

The buzzard bent at his knees and set the gun down nice and easy—feller was smart enough, anyways, to know that throwing it down hard might discharge the thing and kill somebody. Another somebody.

"All right, mister," Tulley told the now-unarmed killer, "you set yourself down at the table there. You, too, señorita. Right now!"

They did so.

"Pedro!" Tulley called out.

The sawed-off guitarist, who was cowering in the corner, trying to hide under his sombrero, called back, "*Qué quieres, señor?*"

"Git the dickens over here."

Pedro got the dickens over there.

Sombrero in hand now, the guitarist asked again, "*Qué quieres?*"

"Go find the sheriff. Should be at the Victory."

"*Si no?*"

"Well, if not, might be in his room at the hotel." Tulley made room for him. "Go!"

Pedro went.

So fast you could hear the dust kick up.

Tulley positioned himself in the doorway again, blocking the way, or, anyway, his scattergun did. Everyone was back in their chairs. The Preacherman and the other varmint that traveled with this Trammel seemed to be going out of their way not to look in his. Cesar, the bartender, also the proprietor, was leaning his elbows on the bar, his folded hands under his chin. He looked bored and kind of put upon.

Pedro did well: within five minutes Caleb York sidled up at Tulley's side. The sheriff patted his deputy on the shoulder, then took a few steps inside. He cast his eyes around the room slowly, then wound up looking down at the dead man but not going over to do so.

"Anyone check him?" York asked.

Heads shook; shoulders shrugged.

"Doesn't look to be breathin'," York admitted. "Cesar, have a look-see."

Cesar came around the bar and went over to kneel by the fallen cowboy. The proprietor's pudgy fingers searched for a pulse in the man's neck. Failing, he looked up at York and said, "*Está muerto*, Sheriff."

York curled a finger, and Cesar came over to him, in no hurry.

"What happened here?" York asked.

Before Cesar answered, the seated Trammel yelled, "It was a fair fight! Nigger drew down on me. He went for it first!"

York looked hard at Cesar.

Cesar smirked and held his hands open. *"Quién sabe?"*

"I will tell you who knows," Alver Hollis said in a calm, commanding voice worthy of a pulpit. He swung around in his chair and gave York a steady, unblinking look. *"I* know. I saw it. Everyone saw it. That black son of a bitch pulled on my friend. It's as clear a case of self-defense as ever was seen on God's green earth."

Twitching half a smile, York said, "How about on indoor straw?"

Hollis stiffened. "That's how it happened."

York pushed his hat on the back of his head. "Is there a Bible verse that covers it, Preacherman?"

"Any number. For example, 'For he is the servant of God, who carries out God's wrath on the wrongdoer.' Romans thirteen, four."

"Somehow I knew it wouldn't be the one about turnin' the other cheek. . . . Anyone else here see anything different?"

Around the room came more head shakes and mumbled negatives.

Tulley slipped up by the sheriff and whispered, "That señorita over there, same table as the troublemaker? *She's* the cause."

York turned his gaze on the girl. "How about it, señorita? Did the cowboy draw first?"

She glanced at Trammel, who was glowering at her, then nodded.

"Positive of that, señorita?"

She swallowed and nodded again.

"Cesar," York said, turning to the proprietor, who remained nearby. "You weren't sure what happened. Are you sure now?"

The big mustachioed head bobbed up and down, then nodded toward the Preacherman. "It was as that one said—as fair a fight as ever I saw. As ever *anyone* saw."

York's grin came slow. "Well, that's good to hear. But I'm afraid we're going to have to close the cantina down for the night. Sorry for the loss of business, Cesar, but somebody's gotta pay for this killing."

Cesar shrugged. A man who ran this kind of place had known for a long time that life was not fair.

"You two," York said, pointing at Hollis and Landrum, "stay put. Need a word. Join your friends, Mr. Trammel. You just leave the gun on the floor there. Everybody else, *out!*"

Tulley stepped outside, and one by one, the patrons piled through. Some went off on foot; others claimed their horses, though a few steeds remained, their owners upstairs with wenches. Others up there had probably fled at the gunshot.

Heading back inside again, Tulley and his double-barrel took their position in the doorway and watched as York strode casually over to the three seated men.

"Mr. Trammel," York said pleasantly, "you seem to have a propensity for trouble."

The bulgy eyes blinked. "A what-sity?"

"A bent toward gettin' yourself in a fix. This is two incidents in one night. Now, it would appear there's no one to stand against you in this shooting."

"He drew on me!"

"So you say. Of course, his gun was in his holster, nice and snug. But he may have made a move. He may. Anyway, I know when I'm buffaloed. You're walkin' out of here a free man."

Hollis said softly, "It *was* self-defense, Sheriff."

"Yeah, I heard you the first time, back when you were directing the choral group in this place in the hymn you wanted sung. Here's the thing. You want to hang around my quiet little town up to and till after the big poker game, fine and dandy. But none of you boys better so much as pass wind, or I'll jail the lot of you. Or worse."

Hollis said, "Is that a threat, Sheriff?"

"Call it a covenant, Preacherman. Now you and your brethren get the hell out of here."

They departed.

York came over to Tulley and said, "Fine job, Deputy. Now go tell Doc Miller to bring a wicker basket for the body."

CHAPTER SEVEN

Early morning sun fell on Willa Cullen's pillow and, when she rolled into it, awoke her from a dream about Caleb York, which vanished, as if scurrying off in embarrassment. She slipped from the comfortable bed, her bare feet kissing the cool wood floor, and went to the dresser to pour water into a basin and wash up.

The bedroom had plenty of windows for sunshine to creep in around the red-and-cream-striped curtains, which were all that remained from her childhood here. Back when her late mother was in charge, this space had been all sweetness and light, ruffles and frills and light colors. What remained was a metal-post double bedstead with a faintly floral spread, a small corner dresser with a water pitcher and lavatory bowl, a hard chair to its left, and a framed desert picture hanging above the bed.

She traded her nightgown for a chemise with drawers, over which her jeans and a green plaid shirt fitted nicely, then—still barefoot—padded out into the kitchen to start breakfast.

Normally, by now, her father would be up and dressed and fixing his own coffee—his blindness had come on gradually enough that certain routines of daily life had carried over without strain. Such things gave Papa a much-needed, if not entirely real, sense of independence. He would be at the small wooden table they usually shared for the morning meal. Today she had in mind eggs and potatoes and bacon and, making use of the cornmeal picked up yesterday at the Mercantile, corn bread.

But there was no sign of him.

She thought perhaps he'd gone off somewhere with Uncle Burt, but their houseguest was still asleep in the extra bedroom. Straw-colored hair loose at her shoulders, she tugged on some boots and went out into the crisp, nearly cold morning air, where she found Whit Murphy sitting on the steps outside the bunkhouse, having a smoke.

On her approach, the lanky foreman got to his feet, tossed his cigarette, and came down to meet her. As he so often did in her presence, Whit took off his hat.

She tried not to be irritable at the man's usual nervousness with her, though she was very tired of it. "Have you seen Papa this morning?"

"Sure did. Saddled up his chestnut and went out ridin' round sunup."

"By *himself*?"

The droopy-mustached face lengthened. "I know you don't like it when he does that, Miss Willa, but I learned a long time ago not to argue with your daddy about such things. He does have his pride."

"You call it pride, Whit, but I call it stubbornness." She drew a deep breath in, let it out slow. "Don't suppose he told you where he was off to . . . ?"

Murphy shook his head. "Just said he cottoned a ride.

But they's only a few places he goes off to alone. You know that, Miss Willa. Uh . . . you need my help?"

"No. No. I'll have a little breakfast, and if he isn't back by then, I'll saddle Daisy up and go out for a ride myself."

She did all that, and when her father still hadn't returned, she set out to find him. Whit was right that there were only a few spots that Papa went off to when he wanted to think and be alone. For a blind man, Papa could take care of himself well enough, but she couldn't countenance his riding off alone.

The banks of the Purgatory River, a tributary of the Pecos, were bordered with lush conifers, and though Papa could no longer see the cold, clear water flowing down from the Sangre de Cristo Mountains, he could surely hear it and smell it and feel it. This was perhaps the most likely place that she would find him.

She hadn't been out this way since she and her late fiancé last picnicked here, and she worried that perhaps her recent reluctance to revisit the spot had encouraged Papa to come out here on his own. But the grassy slope above the sandy, rocky shore where he so often paused on horseback to take the river in showed no signs of him. She rode away from the bittersweet memories as quickly as she could.

The grassy mesas and valleys of the Bar-O were not friendly to a sightless man, even one who owned them. So her next thought was to try the less rolling land where a lone Patriarch Tree ruled, a ways away from a stand of cottonwoods bordering the stream that gave them life.

This magnificent, lonely monarch, its trunk five feet across, nearly one hundred feet tall, had always been a marvel her father relished taking in. He'd been known to dismount and sit beneath the wide branches—as gnarled and reaching as a witch's grasp in winter, yet wearing an autumn shimmer of gold now—and contemplate.

She saw the chestnut first, milling around the tree, nibbling grass, staying in the cooling shade of the cottonwood's spreading crown of bristlecone pine.

As she brought Daisy around, Willa finally spotted her father, sitting as he had so often done with his back to the tree's thick trunk, sitting peacefully, chin on his chest, napping apparently. But as she rode toward him, easily at first, then picking up speed, she realized this was something else.

Something terrible.

When she reached the edge of the golden umbrella of shade, she hopped off Daisy and ran to her father's side and knelt there. She took his hand and squeezed it and said to him, "Papa, Papa, oh, Papa," but her father had nothing to say to his daughter, because he was gone, leaving behind only this small, somewhat sunken version of the big man he'd once been.

He was slumped forward enough that she could see the back of his head, crushed in, a bloody mess, a jagged, irregular window on a brain that no longer thought. On the wood two or three feet above her broken father was a smear of red.

Had the chestnut thrown him?

Had Papa been tossed against the broad multiple trunk of the tree by the animal, spooked possibly by a rattler or some other creature? Possible. But at this moment, the horse seemed docile, munching idly on the grass, unconcerned about the fate of its rider.

She let go of the stiff, cold hand.

Got to her feet.

Did not cry.

She would not do that in front of her father—he had wanted a son and had settled for a strong daughter, and she would not let him down at this late date. Crying could wait till she was home and shut inside her room, the room where she had slept from childhood on, where one of the few times she had previously cried there had been when her mother passed.

Now her father, too, had passed. George Cullen, who had carved out the Bar-O in the face of Indian attacks, bad weather, smallpox, cowpox, and predatory animals of all stripes, including rustlers and marauders. He had taken all that head-on and had triumphed over it, displaying the kind of courage and determination that weren't seen much these days.

Pounding hoofbeats announced that she and her father would not be alone much longer.

In a way that a much younger man might have envied, Burt O'Malley—blue shirt, red bandana, Levi's, Boss of the Plains hat—brought his borrowed dun quarter horse to an abrupt stop and leapt off, then came at Willa at a run, which he brought to just as abrupt a stop upon seeing his dead friend.

"Sweet Jesus, no," O'Malley said as he came up next to Willa and slipped an arm around her shoulder, then hugged her side to his, turning her face away from a sight she had already seen and was seared into her soul.

"Uncle Burt," she said, looking up at him, confused. "However did you find me here?"

He stroked blond tendrils from her face. "Whit told

me you'd gone out looking for your papa. Said this was one of a couple places he'd likely be. Do we know what happened here?"

She nodded toward the nibbling chestnut. "Maybe got thrown somehow?"

O'Malley frowned. "Maybe."

He let go of her and went over for a closer look at his dead partner, pushing his Stetson back, bending down. He glanced up at the smear of red. Shook his head.

"Maybe not," he said.

Coming back over to her, O'Malley said, "One of us should go and get that sheriff friend of yours. I can do it, if you'd rather not stay here with . . . with him."

She squeezed his arm. "No! I *want* to stay. I'll stay with him, all right. You go get Caleb."

He studied her for a few seconds, then nodded, snugged his hat back in place, and remounted the quarter horse. He reined the animal up, then gave her a hard look. "Sure about this?"

"I'm sure," she said.

And he nodded and rode off as hard as if it mattered.

Hat off, jacket off, vest over a gray badge-pinned shirt, Caleb York was seated in his office, going through the latest "wanted" circulars, when Burt O'Malley blew in like a twister. The big man, usually so at ease with himself, leaned both hands against the desktop, breathing hard, shaking.

"George Cullen is dead," he said, choking something back.

York sat forward. "Hell you say? How? When?"

O'Malley gestured vaguely. "Went out ridin' about sunup, foreman says. Daughter found him propped up against a big old cottonwood out on the range. Place he liked to go and sit and think, I gather. But he sure as hell ain't thinkin' now."

"How'd it happen?"

The big man shook his head. "Don't rightly know. Maybe he was throwed. Not sure. Don't quite smell right. Best you take a look."

York got his holstered gun from where it was coiled in a desk drawer. He rose and started buckling it on. "Where's Willa now?"

"With her daddy. That's where she wanted to be." His eyebrows rose. "Why, *you* know a way of keepin' that girl from doin' what she's a mind to?"

"No, sir."

York checked the gun's cylinder—five bullets, an empty chamber under the hammer. Leaving the holster tie-down loose, he went back to the cell where his deputy was sleeping and kicked the cot. Tulley woke like a startled chicken and went for the scattergun propped next to him, but York yanked it away.

York said, "Fetch Doc Miller."

"Can I use the privy first?"

"Yeah, but nothing fancy."

The deputy, who slept in his clothes, started climbing into his boots. York left him there to complete the procedure.

Back in the office, York found O'Malley seated at the rough-hewn table that was generally the deputy's domain; looming over him were wanted posters and a rifle rack, and next to him was the wood-burning stove. The big man seemed small suddenly, hunkered over the table, with his hands folded damn near prayerfully.

York went over to him. Leaned a hand against the table. "Hard to imagine this world without George Cullen in it."

"He was just a blind old man," O'Malley said, looking nowhere. "Past his prime. Good days far behind him."

Then he began to weep.

Ill at ease, York went out onto the boardwalk just in time to see Tulley scurry out from around back, his privy trip over, to head clattering down the boardwalk to Doc Miller's office over the bank.

"*Tulley!*" York called.

The deputy came to so quick a stop, he practically tumbled over himself. He turned and said, "Yes, Sheriff?"

"Tell Doc to bring his buckboard."

"Somethin' to haul?"

"Somethin' to haul."

Tulley resumed his noisy run.

York leaned against a post. He stood there, looking out at Trinidad, wondering if it was cold enough to merit his jacket. This time of day, the town was as peaceful as a Mexican village at siesta. Even the Victory was quiet. Only the occasional random rumble of a wagon or the occasional rhythmic clop of hoofs broke the silence. It was almost as if the town sensed George Cullen's passing and was paying its respects.

The door behind him creaked open, and then O'Malley was beside him.

"An old jailbird like me," the man said, smiling embarrassedly, "shouldn't be so damn sentimental."

York shrugged. "You two went way back. And I understand he treated you right."

O'Malley nodded. "He was a good man. Hell of a man. Could have turned his back on me but instead kept me a partner in his place. Socked money away for me when he never had to. His kind won't pass this way again. The kind that built something out of a wilderness. Kind that made the way for civilization."

Even, York thought, *if he had stood in the way of civilization coming to Trinidad by way of the Santa Fe.*

York asked, "You still staying out at the Bar-O?"

O'Malley nodded. "The old boy wouldn't have it any other way." He frowned. "Think I should move out? Would folks talk, a man stayin' out there with that good-lookin' girl?"

York shook his head. "I think you should stick. She'll need the support. How much emotion did she show?"

"Not as much as me," O'Malley said with a wry chuckle. "Willa's as strong as her old man."

"No," York said, "she isn't. She grew up a daughter living up to her papa's idea of a son. But she's no pioneer. She grew up in a ranch house. Oh, she's strong, all right . . . but she'll still need a shoulder."

O'Malley gave him a long, careful look. "I, uh, somehow gather that maybe you might be the shoulder she'd druther lean on."

"At one time." York shrugged. "But I got on her bad side."

The big man looked at him curiously. "How'd you manage that?"

"Shot and killed her fiancé."

O'Malley's eyebrows rose. "That'll do it," he admitted.

Offering no further explanation, York said, "I know the spot you're talking about, that big old Patriarch Tree. You head back to the Bar-O and hold down the fort there. . . . Here's the Doc now! We can all ride together till you make the turn."

*   *   *

Caleb arrived riding alongside the town doctor, who was at the reins of a rattling buckboard drawn by a single horse, a Missouri Fox Trotter. Half a length ahead of the buckboard, and in much the same way as Uncle Burt had, Caleb brought his gelding to a quick stop and was off the horse in a flash. He went directly to Willa and held her out by the arms and looked at her hard and careful.

His eyes asked her if she was all right, and she nodded. Meanwhile, the pear-shaped doc in the rumpled brown suit got the Gladstone bag off the seat next to him and climbed down from the buckboard in no hurry to make his way to a patient who would never be cured.

Jerking a thumb at the calmly waiting Daisy, Caleb said to Willa, "Maybe you should ride back to the Bar-O. Mr. O'Malley is waitin' there."

She shook her head, and the untended hair was all over the place; she brushed it from her face. "No. I'd like to hear what your thoughts are. And Dr. Miller's."

"Might be a hard thing for you to hear."

Her chin came up. "I have a right. It's my land, and he's my father."

He nodded just a little. "It is. He is. But stay back here a ways. We need to look around a bit. All right?"

"All right."

She went over and stood with Daisy, stroking the horse's snout, while Caleb joined the doctor. They spoke softly, but the breeze carried their voices as the men leaned, one on each side, over her father's remains.

The doctor's voice was gentle, but his words were not. "Rigor mortis has set in. That means two hours, anyway, since he died."

"Could he have been thrown?"

Doc Miller nodded toward the nearby grazing horse. "That chestnut over there is no bronco, but it might be possible. An animal can get spooked. But the bruising on the body here says otherwise."

"That right? Dead bodies talkin' now?"

The doc chuckled grimly. "We've run into this before, Caleb. Look at the purple rising above his collar. I'll wager when I get Mr. Cullen back to my surgery, we'll find his back and backside and the rear of his legs all bruised where the blood settled. If he'd wound up here, sittin' up like this, the blood would've settled only down below."

"You're saying he was moved."

The doc shrugged. "If my assumptions are correct, yes. I don't imagine you want me to strip this gentleman of his clothing and make an examination in the back of my buckboard, just to make sure . . . while his daughter's still in sight."

Caleb said nothing to that. He pointed to the tree trunk overhead. "What about the blood smear?"

"Well, with Mr. Cullen deceased, the blood wouldn't have been flowing . . . but if the corpse was held upright and the head knocked against the tree, some blood would have got there, all right. And, Caleb, that wound does indicate the head took more than one blow."

The doctor leaned her father's head forward a bit for the sheriff to see.

"The death blow," Caleb said, "and then another blow or two, to produce the blood smear?"

"That's right. To make it appear that George Cullen died accidentally. And take a look around. See anything missing?"

"What am I looking for?"

"Pieces of bone. Chunks, even. That's a mighty big hole in the back of that head, Caleb. Now, when I go to digging in my surgery, I'll find shards and such . . . but that leaves a hell of a nasty jigsaw puzzle, one missin' some big pieces."

Caleb sighed. Rose. The flat leaves of the Patriarch were twisting in the breeze, rustling, fluttering, as if tiny birds were hiding in the gnarled branches under their golden covering. He had a look around on the ground where his own footsteps and those of Willa, O'Malley, and the doctor had broken twigs and left impressions.

But there were also signs of something having been dragged across the grass—consistent with the doctor's thoughts on the body having been moved, brought here to this lonely place to provide an accidental explanation for what must have occurred. . . .

"Murder, then," Caleb said.

A chill went through Willa, far colder than the breeze riffling the leaves.

Pointing out the flattened area where the body might have been dragged to the tree and propped up, Caleb said, "It may have been brought in a wagon."

He followed the path of the pressed-down grass and found the impressions of wagon wheels at the edge of the shaded area. The doctor came over and joined him.

"Murder," Caleb said again.

"That's my preliminary diagnosis, Sheriff," Doc Miller said. "And it's not like you're gonna be shy of motives."

Caleb shook his head. "Not hardly. Refusing to sell land to the railroad for their branchline as he did? Standing in the way of fortunes being made? George Cullen had no shortage of enemies."

And with her father gone, Willa realized, that left her

in charge of the Bar-O . . . and the decision making where accommodating the railroad was concerned.

Caleb came over to her, hat in hand. "You were listening, of course."

"I was listening, of course."

"Burt O'Malley and me are in agreement that it's best he stay on at the Bar-O for now. You might need some help in the days ahead, and like they say, he's the O in the Bar-O."

"*I'm* the Bar-O," she said.

His smile came gentle. "I know you are . . . now. But your *father* was the Bar-O till somebody killed him—probably somebody who wants to see that branchline go in, meaning you are going to get leaned on in ways you can't begin to picture."

Again, her chin came up. "I can take of myself."

"Your father thought that, too, but he was wrong. People in this part of the country like to say they can stand alone. Take care of things all by themselves. But the truth of it is, we can't. All of us need somebody."

Was he saying he needed her?

"Anyway," he said, snugging on the cavalry pinch hat, "it's up to you. Your ranch, your land, hell, your cows. Throw the old boy out on his tail if you like."

With a shrug, she said, "Uncle Burt can stay awhile."

"Good. But you need to head back there long about now. The doc and I have to deal with your late father. He's evidence now, and I need him and the doc's help to find the bastard that did this to somebody we both loved."

He tipped his hat, nodded, and went back to help the doctor. Framed by the massive tree trunk, the two men stood beside her seated father and waited for her to go so she didn't have to see Papa hauled to the buckboard like a sack of grain and flung in.

She got on Daisy and rode at a good clip, but her mind was racing even faster, thinking about how she'd kept from her father how she really felt about the spur.

But whom had she shared it with?

And was she indirectly responsible for her father's death?

CHAPTER EIGHT

On the second floor of the formidable brick bank building, Dr. Albert Miller maintained a two-room office—waiting area and surgery—behind which were his living quarters.

Caleb York had helped the doctor up the outer stairs with the wicker-basket-laden body of George Cullen and into the smallish surgery, where they had transferred it to the heavy mahogany examination table. On its back, the stiffened corpse remained clothed, a condition the doctor began to remedy.

York, his mood melancholy, hung up his hat on the coat tree by the door, then sat and waited at a desk cluttered with books, papers, and bottles, a spittoon on the floor nearby. On the walls, framed diplomas hung crookedly, and overseeing everything from a corner was a skeleton, referred to by Miller as Hippocrates, who, York gathered, was a famous Greek doctor and whose actual skeleton this likely wasn't.

The doctor said, "Help me turn him over."

Caleb went and did that, not all the way over, just enough to see that Doc's diagnosis at the scene had been right: the postmortem bruising was along Cullen's back, from his neck down through his legs and buttocks, confirming the victim had fallen on his back, which indicated he'd been killed elsewhere.

The doc covered Cullen's body with a sheet but for the man's head, propping it up with a folded towel to provide a better look at that large, ragged, nasty wound. He got some tools from a cabinet and began poking. York watched. A good ten minutes passed.

Doc, bloody medical tools in his hands, gave York a steady look. "As I thought—not enough skull fragments to put Humpty Dumpty back together. You got yourself a murder, all right."

York nodded. "Keep it to yourself for now, Doc. Don't want it gettin' around till I've talked to some folks. Any idea when he died?"

"Whit Murphy saw him ride out around sunup. The old man had been dead at least two hours before I got to him. I'd say between six thirty and nine or so?"

Harris Mercantile was doing a good business, women in calico or gingham with bonnets, often with their young children, moving through the gloomy chamber with its high-shelved walls, navigating floors crammed with boxes, barrels, and crates. They would pause to riffle through the piled clothing on the facing counters or, short of that, go looking wide-eyed through the big mail-order catalogs.

At the cash register behind the counter at right, where he could also tend the coffee grinder and scales, was Newt Harris himself, the blond, heavyset proprietor in a dark bow tie and a light-colored vest. His jaw was bruised from where a blind man had hit him.

"Sheriff," he said with a nod, dark blue eyes wary.

"Mr. Harris," York said, returning the nod. "Might I have a word?"

"Certainly, if you can tolerate the occasional interruption." His smile tried to be pleasant but came off forced. "These *are* business hours."

"I'm workin', too," York said cheerfully. "I was wondering if you and George Cullen had patched things up. I know you been friends for years, and it's too bad about that dustup between you two . . . and that it spilled over between your boy Lem and that friend of Mr. Cullen's."

Bristling, Harris said, "You should arrest that O'Malley galoot. Picking on a kid like Lem!"

Lem could have lifted a horse and tossed it down the street, but York let that pass.

"How about it?" York asked. "Where do things stand with you and George Cullen?"

Big shoulders shrugged. "Well, the same, I'd have to say. I haven't spoken to him since that unpleasantness. If anybody's owed an apology, it's me, and, anyway, I have no use for that stubborn coot. Standing in the way of progress. He's a fool!"

"If so," York said, "he's a dead one."

Harris reared back a shade, his eyes so wide, there was white all around.

Quietly, so as not to be overheard, York briefly told the merchant what had happened—that apparently, what was meant to be written off as an accident had really been murder.

They paused while Harris took care of a customer, a mother buying some printed cotton for a dress for her young daughter.

By the time the bell over the door rang with the mother and child's departure, Harris's bluster had disappeared. His face was somber; his eyes were tearing up.

"You've shamed me, Sheriff, but I had it comin'. George Cullen was a longtime good friend, and whatever recent disagreements we may have had, I would never wish him any harm, much less . . . He was a fine, fine man. If . . . if you'll excuse me. . . ."

The merchant, digging a handkerchief from his pocket, turned his back to York. Muffled sniffling, followed by a nose-blowing honk, preceded a red-eyed Harris turning back to York.

"I . . . I appreciate you telling me, Sheriff. But why didn't you come right out with it? Why ask me if I had mended fences with . . . ? Oh. Oh."

"Yes, Mr. Harris. You had a public altercation with the deceased the day before his murder. Comes down to that."

Stiffly, he said, "I'm not the kind of man that kills another."

"Nobody is till it happens. Where were you around sunup?"

His nod indicated the apartment above. "Upstairs with my wife and my two boys. Lem and Luke are working out back. You can talk to them. Lucille is at her prayer group at the church. You can talk to them all. But I'd appreciate you doing so discreetly. My family needn't know that I'm a . . ."

"Suspect, no. They needn't know that. Anyone *not* in your family who might back you up?"

Harris frowned. "You don't trust me, Sheriff?"

York gave him an easy grin. "I trust myself and no one else when there's a murder and no clear culprit."

The merchant swallowed thickly. "Well . . . we opened at nine. We've had a nice steady flow of customers. I could probably make you a list, if need be. I know them all."

"Why don't you do that? I'll send Deputy Tulley around to pick it up this afternoon."

York tugged his hat in good-bye and left. That list wouldn't be necessary, most likely, but he didn't mind putting the man out one bit.

The Davis Apothecary, with its big jars of brightly colored liquid in the window, was perhaps a third the size of the Mercantile, though no less impressive with its elaborate dark-oaken cabinetry of wall-to-wall drawers and shelving, the latter displaying gold rim–labeled, glass-stoppered bottles of various sizes and colors—dark blue, amber, clear—as well as tins and jars.

The local druggist was something of a master of his craft, growing medicinal herbs out back, including sassafras and Virginia snakeroot. Those added to the distinctive spicy aroma in the air. Along a waist-high shelf were fine tools and trays used to make pills; on the counter at right, a brass pestle and mortar. Behind the counter was Clement Davis.

The skinny, bug-eyed, weak-jawed druggist wore a white apron over his vest with a bow tie, above which a prominent Adam's apple bobbed as he said, "Good morning, Sheriff. Something I can help you with?"

No customers were on hand to slow the interview down, so York got right to it. He pushed his hat back on his head and, in a friendly but professional way, asked, "Just how ticked are you with George Cullen, Clem?"

The bluntness of that brought the druggist's natural nervousness to the fore. York had always wondered how so timid a creature was able to summon a steady hand for the making of pills with their rigorous recipes.

"I, uh, well, I have no *problem* with Mr. Cullen," Davis said, wiggling his fingers. "He has a right to his opinion, however much I might disagree with him."

"You were part of that Citizens Committee group that confronted him last night."

"Well, as a member of the committee, I, uh, certainly *needed* to be there . . . to represent the town's interests and, uh, well, my own. Nothing wrong with that."

"Nothing a'tall," York agreed. "But there *was* pressure bein' applied."

The chin came up, and the Adam's apple followed. "I don't see any reason why there shouldn't be friendly discussion with the old man. No reason not to, uh, show him gentle like the error of his thinking. That spur will mean the *world* to this town!"

York nodded. "Your business would surely benefit."

The bug eyes blinked and blinked. "And what would be wrong with that?"

"Nothing." York leaned an elbow on the counter. "Have you had any private conversations with George Cullen on the subject?"

His chin was quivering, like that of a child about to burst into tears. "No. No, but I'm confident he *will* come around."

York's half smirk had no humor in it. "Why would you think that, Clem?"

Eyebrows rose. "Well, I, uh . . . don't know if I should say, exactly. It's something the mayor told me in confidence."

"Okay, then. I'll check with him. Wouldn't want you to

break a confidence. What time did you open up this morning, Clem?"

Knobby shoulders shrugged. "A tad late. I had to run some morphine pills out to the McLaughlin place. Got the dysentery out there."

"When was that?"

"First thing. I rode out there around seven. By the time I got back and opened up, it was past nine thirty."

The McLaughlin place was in the opposite direction of the Bar-O.

"They'll back you up, the McLaughlins?"

More blinking. "Of course. But . . . but why should they *have* to?"

"Because George Cullen was murdered this morning, sometime between sunup and nine."

York nodded and went out, leaving the druggist frozen behind him, Adam's apple in mid-rise.

York's next stop was the smallest of the storefronts, with its red-and-white pole and window painted with bold white letters:

BARBERSHOP
MAYOR JASPER P. HARDY
PROPRIETOR
HAIRCUT 10 CENTS, SHAVE 5 CENTS.

Within, York found the undersized mayor in his typical white jacket with black bow tie, his slicked-back black hair and perfect handlebar mustache his own best advertising. Right now he was brushing clippings off the cape of his latest patron, telegraph manager Ralph Parsons, a scrawny, bespectacled soul for whom good grooming could do only a limited amount.

The space was home to a single, if fancy chair—carved oak with padded red-leather upholstery—and a big walnut-framed mirror over a marble counter lined with colorful blown-glass tonic bottles. The floor was bare wood planking; the side wall bore a Winchester hunting-scene calendar, a doorless cupboard of shaving mugs, and an assortment of nicely hand-lettered signs (SHAVING, LEECHING, BLEEDING and HOT & COLD BATHS). A few empty chairs along the rear wall waited for further customers.

York traded nods with Parsons on his way out, while the barber beamed at this potential customer.

"What's your pleasure this morning, Sheriff?"

York settled into the chair as the barber/mayor covered him with a fresh cape. "Just a shave, Your Honor. The hair can wait till next week."

Hardy was a pretty fair barber, and York just sat and enjoyed the ritual for a while, the hot towel, the brush whipping in its cup, and the lather applied. Not until Hardy was actually scraping the straight razor across his face did York risk a question between strokes.

"When did you open up this morning, Jasper?" No "Your Honor" this time.

The blade rose expertly up York's right cheek.

"Right at eight, Sheriff. Always have a few customers who want a fresh shave before their shops open."

Which was 9:00 a.m. in most cases, earlier for the Mercantile and the hardware store.

In the next pause, York asked, "And before that?"

The mayor, who was unmarried, usually took his breakfast at the hotel or at the café, and York, who had eaten at the former this morning, hadn't seen him there.

Another stroke of the blade. He was starting on York's

throat now, his customer's chin up. "Breakfast at the café. Why do you ask, Sheriff?"

At the next pause, York said, "I'll get to that. How have you been getting along with Old Man Cullen lately?"

The barber continued the tender work—he rarely nicked a client. "We've always been friendly. I like the man. I believe he likes me. This current disagreement is just a passing thing. He'll come around."

"Why do you say that?"

"I just know he will, that's all." Hardy smiled to himself. "Anyway, I have a good *idea* he will."

York said nothing more till the cape was whipped off and he'd given the barber a nickel and a grin. "Sure like to know the reason you're so sure George Cullen will come to his senses 'bout Trinidad's future and all."

Hardy hesitated, then gestured to his fancy chair. "Well, it's something the old man told me, seated right there. He said his own daughter was against him in the fight. I know the old boy well enough to figure he'll buckle under to her. She's all but running the ranch now herself, and he damn well knows it."

"Jasper, I happen to know Willa hasn't said a word to her papa about the way she really feels where the branchline is concerned."

A big smile blossomed under the elaborate mustache. "That's *how* he knows! Normally, she'd be fighting at his side. She kept mum, and that spoke volumes. What's going on, Sheriff? What's this about?"

York told him.

The news of Cullen's death staggered the barber, who stumbled back into his own chair and sat, mouth hanging open, as if his jaw were broken.

"I . . . I can't believe it," he said softly. "Such a great man. There wouldn't *be* a Trinidad without him. It's a tragedy, Sheriff. It's a goddamned tragedy! You'll find the one who did this. I *know* you will."

"I know it, too," York said, stroking his chin. "Nice and smooth. Thanks, Your Honor."

Mathers & Sons Hardware was similar in size and layout to the Mercantile, its windows promising seeds, farm implements, and household supplies. Floor-to-ceiling ladders ran on rails on either side for the higher shelves. You could buy nails by the pound here or a single nut and bolt. You could order a buggy from Denver and, out in back, purchase harnesses, hay, and grain. Buckets and pails and small barrels hung from the ceiling, as if gravity had changed its mind.

The scent of the place made York smile—oiled metal, tobacco, mineral spirits, and wood. It smelled like men getting things done. Still, though this was Mathers & Sons, the fleshy, fifty-some proprietor had only one son, and, in fact, his daughter Margaret, in her late teens, did the books and helped with the ordering.

From behind the counter, where his boy was running the register, the bald but lavishly mutton-chopped Clarence Mathers, an apron over his gray suit, greeted the sheriff with a smile and an extended hand. York reached over the counter to accept it. The clientele, running to ranchers and their employees and, of course, some town folk, was just thick enough in here that York suggested he and Mathers step out onto the boardwalk.

This they did, taking two of the waiting chairs lined up in front of the store; no others were taken.

"Had any words with George Cullen," York said, "over this spur wrangle?"

"Well, I wouldn't call it a wrangle," the good-humored merchant said. "Difference of opinion. And I understand it. George sees things through his end of the telescope, and we see them through ours."

"But you think he's mistaken."

He pawed the air. "Oh, my, yes. Got his head up his hindquarters on this one. Sure, it'll hurt his spread for a time, but as things expand around here, the Bar-O will thrive more than ever."

Nothing was said for maybe half a minute.

Then York offered, "Lovely day."

"Very nice. Little cool, but I like it crisp."

"As do I. What time did you open up this morning, Clarence?"

The merchant smiled. "Well, actually, I didn't. My daughter and that boy of mine in there did. They're starting to make me feel as useless as teats on a boar. You know, that girl has an equal share in my will. I believe if she finds the right man, she'll be the one carrying this hardware store into the next century."

"Where were *you* then?"

"I took the wagon out."

"Really? Where to?"

"I had supplies to deliver to the Circle G. Why?"

The Circle G was in the general area of the Bar-O, but not close enough to make this admission anything for York to sit up about.

York asked, "Folks out there back you up?"

"Of course. But why the hell would they need to?"

York told him.

The big fleshy man slumped in his chair. His face went bloodless, and he was shaking his head, staring at the planks underfoot.

Mathers's voice was hushed. "Murdered, you say? Hell of a thing. Hell of a terrible thing. We wouldn't have a town without that man! This part of the country would be Indians and wild animals without the likes of him! Who would *do* such a thing?"

"I was thinking maybe one of your brother merchants on the Citizens Committee."

His eyes and nostrils flared. "Not a chance in Hades! We had a dispute, yes, but we were all friends. No one can deny that. He was *on* the committee, for Lord's sake!"

"He stood in the way of progress. Of commerce."

"He'd have come around."

"Because his daughter would have stood against him?"

That surprised Mathers. "I . . . I didn't say that. Where did you hear that?"

York didn't answer. He stood and said, "You have any further thoughts on this subject, Clarence, I'd be obliged if you shared them."

He left the man there, still seated in front of his storefront windows, staring bleakly at his feet and the wood beneath them—the wood of a boardwalk his nails held together.

The office of the *Trinidad Enterprise* was at the church end of Main, in a narrow two-story clapboard building the color of butter, brand new and nestled next to the saddle shop.

York went in and was immediately hit with the oily smell of ink. Editor Oscar Penniman, in gartered shirtsleeves and a black visor, sat at his rolltop desk against the right wall, hunkered over a torn-off sheet of foolscap, writing in pencil.

At a table at left, Penniman's young aproned assistant, Harold Jones, a Kansas City import, whom York had spoken to only once or twice, sat arranging type by hand in little metal trays. Against the wall were four five-foot narrow-drawer typeset cabinets.

Toward the rear, and consuming much of the space, was a cast-iron and wood contraption as big as a buckboard, with a central drum, levers, gears, and springs. Silent now, the printing press looked like it could make a hell of a racket in motion, like some ancient beast that might come lumbering toward you.

No bell over the door had announced York, but the editor soon sensed his presence, anyway, and turned toward him with a guarded smile, a nod, and "Sheriff."

"Mr. Penniman. I have a story for you."

"Come. Take a seat." A smile flickering under the perfectly trimmed mustache, he gestured to a nearby chair, which York went over and filled.

"I admit I'm surprised to see you, Sheriff. I rather got the impression that your opinion of me and my paper was, well, less than entirely favorable."

"I really have no opinion either way," York said. "But it does seem a bit on the shady side that you don't advertise your silent partner."

"What silent partner would that be?" the editor asked too innocently.

"The Santa Fe Railroad. But we've covered that. And, anyway, if I have a story that needs putting in front of the public, where else could I go but the *Enterprise*?"

Penniman studied the sheriff for a moment, then shrugged and grabbed a new piece of paper, pencil poised. "All right, then. What news is it you have for our readers?"

"George Cullen has been murdered."

The editor stiffened, looking up from the as yet un-written-upon paper. "Well, that's a shock. *Terrible* to hear. You're . . . you're sure of this?"

York nodded, then gave him a superficial account, just the bare facts and none of the doctor's medical opinions.

Penniman frowned. "But . . . that sounds as if he was thrown from his horse . . . ?"

York gestured to Penniman's paper.

Then he said, " 'Sheriff Caleb York, formerly a detective with Wells Fargo, considers the circumstances highly suspicious and is handling the tragedy as a murder investigation. The body apparently was moved and arranged to suggest accidental death. The deceased's reluctance to support the Santa Fe Railroad's proposed branchline, the sheriff says, is a possible motive.' You get all that?"

Hunkered over again, Penniman was still writing. Then he said, "I got it. Want to hear it?"

"Yes."

The editor read it back. He had it word for word.

"You're talking to possible suspects, I assume," Penniman said.

"Yes. For example, where were you this morning between sunup and ten?"

The editor straightened a little. "So I'm a suspect, then?"

"You and the Santa Fe Railroad . . . but you don't have to quote that if you aren't so inclined. Where were you, Mr. Penniman? This morning?"

The editor's dark eyes flared. "Right here! You can talk to Mr. Jones there, and he'll confirm it. I took an early breakfast at the hotel and was at the office by seven thirty."

"Mr. Jones might be inclined to back up his boss."

"What, and risk being charged as a murder accomplice? Sheriff, based upon what you've said, I would need a buckboard to accomplish this foul deed, one of which I do *not* own. Here, I don't even own a horse. And the only place I could have rented either buckboard or steed would be the livery, and you can check there and find that I didn't."

York nodded, rose. "I'll do that. Add to the story, if you please, that the sheriff would appreciate any information about this possible murder that your readers might be able to share. All right, sir?"

Penniman frowned—almost scowled—but he nodded before returning to his foolscap.

The front windows of the next business Caleb York visited displayed two well-crafted mahogany caskets with brass fittings and a small dignified sign that said:

C. P. PERKINS
CABINETMAKER
& UNDERTAKER.

Such fancy coffins were only for those well-off citizens to whom life, if not death, had been kind. This display at times had made way for the remains of such outlaws as the late sheriff Harry Gauge and various members of the Rhomer clan, who'd had a grudge against the current sheriff.

If York ever ended up on the wrong end of a gunfight, he knew his next stop would surely be this window.

York entered into a showroom of sorts, with less ostentatious caskets at right and various cabinets, dressers, tables, and chairs at left—death on one hand, life on the other. A desk off in a corner was not for sale; this was Undertaker Perkins's work area, though he was not seated there. Hammering from in back sent York in that direction.

The back room was a workshop, with stacked lumber, a tool-strewn workbench, and the smell of sawdust. The barn-style doors at the rear of the building allowed the storing of a funeral wagon, its black, feathery plumes and glass windows protected by a tarpaulin. Skinny, bald, mustached Perkins, without his usual Abe Lincoln high hat, looked even smaller than he usually did. But in his BVD top he showed off a surprising musculature as he hammered away at his latest creation.

On a nearly upright wooden framework—almost certainly the undertaker's own work—the coffin in progress rested as he nailed its pieces together. This was a strictly functional pine box, a world—a lifetime—away from the brass-fitted eternal beds in the window.

Perkins had not seen him step in, and York waited for a pause in the hammering before announcing himself.

"Adding some inventory, Mr. Perkins?"

A ghost of a smile flickered on the solemn face as he looked back at York. "There could be a need."

"Because of the Preacherman and the two sinners he rides with?"

Another ghostly smile. "A possibility, wouldn't you say?"

"No question."

Perkins set down his hammer on a small battered table and came over to York, who was only a few paces into the workshop. "What brings you around, Sheriff? I don't imagine you came to window-shop."

"No. I'd be fine with one of these pine boxes. No need for anything fancy, considerin' the destination."

The slight yet muscular figure shrugged. "A man of practical considerations. But I'm pleased your attitude isn't widely held. The more civilized men become, the more they want to go out in style."

"I stopped by to tell you that you have a new customer. He's over in Doc Miller's surgery."

"Ah," he said solemnly. "Someone I know?"

This wasn't as facetious as it might sound: few of the many cowhands on the surrounding spreads would be familiar to the undertaker, although everyone in the town proper would.

York told Perkins about Cullen's passing, including that he believed it to be murder and why.

"And you," the undertaker said, "are assuming those of us who challenged him last night regarding his wrongheaded views about the Santa Fe spur are key suspects. And that would include me."

"It would."

Another shrug, more elaborate this time. "I have no alibi. No wife or children, and I work here alone."

York gestured to the covered funeral wagon. "And you also have a ready means of transportation."

"Without horses," Perkins said with a sly smile, "I most certainly do not. And if you haven't checked at the livery already, you'll find when you do that I haven't rented any horses in some weeks. Will that suffice as an alibi, Sheriff?"

"Guess it will have to," York said and took his leave, while the undertaker returned to his hammering.

After all, even a man as brave as Caleb York didn't find much to like about hanging around an establishment like this.

CHAPTER NINE

Willa Cullen—in the same plaid shirt, jeans, and boots in which she'd found her dead father under a tree a few hours before—led her calico, Daisy, to the grooming stall in the horse barn. Daisy was good about not wandering away, but Willa tied the animal up, anyway.

The barn was cool but not cold, and she had it to herself—stable hand Lou Morgan was off exercising her papa's buggy ponies, which didn't get used every day. She supposed the stable smell would have put some females off, but she rather relished the unique aroma of various parts leather, hay, grain, manure, urine, mud, grass, wood, and tack polish.

She filled her mind with nothing but tending to her tricolored pinto, white with black and brown spots, white mane, brown tail. A curry brush, moved in a circular manner, loosened up the dirt on Daisy's coat, but the brush was too coarse for the animal's face.

The loping jangle of spurs and the crunch of boots on hay announced the approach of unwanted company. The last thing she needed right now was sympathy or talk of what next. But she understood that wish was unrealistic, and smiled back at Whit Murphy, hoping it didn't look forced.

"Morning, Whit," she said. "It *is* still morning, isn't it?"

The foreman, high-beamed Carlsbad hat in hand, came to a stop a respectful distance away and stood outside the stall, slumped, head hanging, his whole face, his whole body as droopy as his mustache. The work shirt, bandana, and shotgun chaps seemed to hang on him like laundry on a line.

"You needn't trouble yourself with such work, time like this, Miss Willa. I can give Lou a holler. He'll give that little pinto any attention she might crave."

Willa smiled faintly as she continued brushing. "I'm not troubling myself, Whit. I'm keeping my mind off things. Keeping busy."

He took a tentative step forward. "I just want you to know, Miss Willa, that iffen there's any way I can help . . . anything a'tall I can do . . ."

People always said such things at times like this. But what could Whit Murphy do to help? What was there that *anyone* could do?

Still, she knew Whit wasn't just another friendly acquaintance, trying to say the right thing—Whit had almost been like a son to her daddy. She and Papa couldn't have run the ranch half as well without him after the rancher's eyesight failed.

Nor was she unaware that the shy cowpoke was sweet on her.

"Just keep things runnin' nice and smooth, Whit," she told him. "The way Papa would want it."

She used a dandy brush to remove dirt from Daisy's coat in quick, short strokes in the direction of the hair, flicking off dirt from the calico's coat. Daisy just stood there, basking in the attention, giving up not a whinny, just the occasional proud shake of the head.

When Whit spoke again, she was almost surprised he was still there.

He said, "Would you like me to ride into town, Miss Willa, and talk to Reverend Caldwell? Make arrangements and all?"

That almost irritated her. In what world did such things fall to a ranch foreman? But she knew he only wanted to help.

"No," she said. "This afternoon I'll ride in and see the reverend myself. Not looking to have a service at Missionary Baptist, just a graveside gathering."

It would have to be soon. Undertaker Perkins did not have embalming available, like some Civil War–trained members of his trade. She shivered at the thought of her father being just so much meat that would soon spoil.

"Thank you, though, Whit. You're kind."

She smiled at him again and nodded in a way that tried to tell him nicely that this conversation was over. But he lingered, turning the hat in his hands like a wheel.

"Don't you worry yourself none," he told her. "I'll keep the Bar-O runnin' steady till, uh . . . till you get around to makin' your mind up."

She frowned at Daisy's side, but any crossness was gone when she glanced back at the cowhand again. "Make it up about what, Whit?"

His head remained lowered, but his eyes gazed up at her, like those of a dog fearing a swat from its mistress. "Whether or not to sell the Santa Fe right of passage for that there branchline."

She kept brushing. "You have an opinion?"

"Is it my place to?"

"You as much as anybody."

His chin came off his chest. "I say stick with what your daddy wanted. You know what his wishes was. Otherwise the Santa Fe wins."

Now she looked right at him. "It's not a contest, is it?"

"No, ma'am, but the way I see it, it's our way of life against theirs."

"How so?"

"Well, like your papa said, it'd give the competition a leg up and turn little Trinidad into Sodom or Gomorrah."

She managed not to smile. "Well, we wouldn't want that, would be, Whit?"

"No, miss."

He gave her a shy, respectful nod, tugged the hat on, and shuffled off, spurs jingling. Then she heard him stop, say, "Sir," and move on. She stepped out of the stall for a look, and big Burt O'Malley was approaching, that lazy, loping way of his compromised by an expression clenched with concern.

"Uncle Burt," she said with a nod and returned to the stall and her work.

With a body brush, Willa began applying long, even strokes to Daisy's coat, smoothing out her hair, getting off any residue of dirt.

O'Malley was at the mouth of the stall now, arms folded, a grave expression carved into the oblong, salt-and-pepper-bearded face. "That help, child? Workin' yourself to a frazzle like that?"

Her eyes were on her efforts. "You prefer I go cry my eyes out in my room?"

"Might," he admitted, approaching. "Might. Bottlin' it up won't do you a lick of good. You don't let sorrow out, it festers."

Her back was to him. "I don't see what good crying would do. If I was a son, not a daughter, would you say such things to me?"

Daisy's coat was getting nice and shiny.

"I believe I would," O'Malley said. "A son *would* cry. Behind closed doors, maybe. But grieving is natural. Not a male or female thing."

"I'll do it in my own way, then."

He drew closer but didn't crowd her. She was using a mane comb now, untangling Daisy's tail. Such work required a gentleness, and she sometimes paused to use her fingers for untangling.

The big man said, "I overheard some of what Whit had to say."

"Did you? Eavesdropping doesn't become a man. More a woman's thing, don't you think?"

Why did she feel so angry? Why was she treating Uncle Burt like this?

But O'Malley ignored her rudeness. "*You're* the Bar-O now, Willa. Your father didn't have a son, so a daughter'll have to do. Whit's opinion ain't worth spit. Mine neither. It's all down to you, girl."

She shifted to a dandy brush to bring further softness to Daisy's tail, but she dropped the thing in the process. O'Malley was right there to pick it up and hand it to her, both of them on their haunches, looking right at the other.

They stood.

The irritation was out of her tone as she said, "I'm in a bad place, Uncle Burt."

He placed a gentle hand on her shoulder. "Of course you are, child. I ain't in the sunshine my own self. All these years and I finally get my old partner back, and now he's lost to me forever. Ain't nohow easy."

She sighed. Moved away, returning to Daisy. She kept working, and O'Malley just stood and watched. She used the brush on the animal's mane, and the beast almost purred. Finally, she began cleaning Daisy's hooves, standing next to her, bending, and supporting one hoof at a time. With a hoof pick, she worked out rocks and turf there, scraping away from herself, not particularly wanting any of that stuff to get flung in her face.

"You know your way around horseflesh," O'Malley said.

"I should. I lived on this ranch all my life. Was riding before I could walk."

"You want to tell me?"

"Tell you what?"

"Why it is you're in a 'bad place.' I don't mean losing your daddy. I mean the position that losin' your daddy has put you in."

She leaned against the side of the stall. He came over and leaned in next to her, their backs to the wood.

"I never told Papa," she said, almost whispering, as if her late parent might overhear, "but we didn't see eye to eye on the Santa Fe spur."

He frowned, studying her. "You mean . . . you were in *favor* of it?"

She nodded. "No reason not to be. You can't keep the future from your door. Times change whether you want 'em to or not."

"No kiddin'," the big man said with a grin and a deep chuckle. "I hardly recognized the Bar-O when that buckboard brought me out here. Trouble was, I think, once his outside vision left him, your papa's inside vision left him, too. By which I mean his ability to see the possibilities that lay ahead."

She looked at him curiously. "I thought you were on Daddy's side of this, Uncle Burt. Heard you tell him myself how you agreed with him about blocking the spur."

His grin wore embarrassment. "Would you think less of me, child, if I admitted I told him what he *wanted* to hear? Last thing I was after was to ride in and get on the wrong side of that beautiful, stubborn old man."

"You wanted your friendship back."

He nodded. "I wanted my friendship back. I'd have stood with him on any side of about any issue he wanted me to. Some of that was selfish. Your papa was my way into respectability after wastin' so much of my life behind bars."

She shook her head. "You didn't have to play that game with him, Uncle Burt. He would have been glad to help, in any case. Like *I'll* be glad to help."

Something pixieish came into the white-beard-framed smile. "Well, then, why don't we put that Cullen/O'Malley partnership back together, girl? Instead of sellin' me one of them smaller spreads, let me sink all that money your daddy put away for me back into the Bar-O itself."

"Uncle Burt . . ."

He raised a gentle hand. "Now hear me out. With George Cullen gone, don't you think Willa Cullen could use a strong male right hand? And I don't mean Whit Murphy, who makes a decent foreman, I'm sure, but is sure as hell no George Cullen, forgive my language."

Almost irritated again, she asked, "But you *are*?"

He shook his head once, firmly. "No. Nobody could replace your daddy. But I could be right there beside you, with some helpful words and a strong arm . . . and besides which, these fools that can't accept a woman like yourself runnin' things? My presence might smooth things out a bit for 'em."

She gave him an unblinking gaze. "I intend to run this ranch myself, Uncle Burt."

"And if you want me to be a part of things, you still *would* be. I'd be your ramrod here at the ranch, and I don't mean just on cattle drives. Anyway, I'm only offerin' this as somethin' you might consider. You don't see me as part of the Bar-O, I'll be more than happy with that little spread you and your daddy picked out for me."

Of course, Burt O'Malley was the O in Bar-O. . . .

"It's kind of you, Uncle Burt. But let me think on it some."

"Naturally."

She sighed. "Papa dying means I can do what I want where that railroad right of passage goes."

"That's so."

"But that troubles me most of all."

"Why?"

She mulled it a few moments. Was it all right to talk of this before it became public? Well, it would be out there soon enough. . . .

"Papa was murdered," she said.

O'Malley lurched forward from where he'd been leaning beside her on the wooden stall frame. Turned to look directly at her. "So he wasn't thrown."

"He wasn't thrown. We just saw something that we were supposed to take that way."

She shared with O'Malley what she'd overheard when Caleb and Doc Miller, doing their detective work, had been talking over her father's body.

"Murdered," O'Malley said, tasting the word and not

at all liking the flavor. "Why in hell? Because . . . because of his stand on the *spur*, you think?"

She sighed. "Must be. No one else had any grudge against him. But if he was killed to clear the path for that branchline, I can't in good conscience go along with the Santa Fe's efforts. Doesn't matter that he and I were on opposite sides of the thing—I *have* to honor his wishes."

Nodding slowly, O'Malley asked, "Did you tell anybody that you and your papa were on opposite sides of the spur?"

"No."

He shrugged. "Then how can you think he was killed to put you in charge of the decision? That's what you're sayin', isn't it?"

"I guess maybe it is."

"Could be whoever killed your daddy had some other motive entirely."

"Possible. Possible." She drew in a breath deep, let it out slow. "Which means I shouldn't jump to a decision. I should wait."

"Wait for what?"

"Well, for one thing, wait for Caleb York to bring in whoever killed my father."

Late morning, Caleb York found Trinidad's modest barrio its usual mix of languid and lively, the dusty path between facing adobes filled with yapping dogs, clucking chickens, and squalling children. The smell of beans frying came through windows where *las madres* could be glimpsed, their men off doing servile work in town or perhaps tending a small patch of land behind their humble homes.

At the end of this tumbledown lane, the two-story

Cantina de Toro Rojo was looking less grand by day, minus music and glowing windows and señoritas for sale, just a bigger adobe version of its neighbors. No horses were tied up out front; no one was coming in or out. The place might have been deserted.

York went through the arched doorless door and found the place empty but for the proprietor, Cesar, who was cleaning blood off the wall in the aftermath of last night's gunfight, fading the bullfight mural further.

The sweaty, hooded-eyed fat man—halfhearted strands of black hair atop his round head, scraggly bandito mustache, and untucked cream-colored shirt with matching trousers—put down his bucket and tossed a sodden rag into it with a plop.

"You always welcome here, Sheriff," Cesar said in a weary monotone at odds with his words, "but you know we don't open till sundown."

What Cesar said was not strictly true—men from the barrio might wander in here during daylight for a tequila or a beer. But the Red Bull was not the kind of place white men frequented before dark, at least not in Trinidad.

"Just looking for a word, Cesar."

York crunched across the straw-covered floor and took a seat near the owner and his bucket.

"Those three gringos last night," York said lazily, arms folded, leaning back, "the little group includin' the one that messed up your wall . . . what became of them?"

Cesar thought about that. It was clear several answers to that question floated in the fat man's head, perhaps even an honest one, but he seemed to be having trouble selecting one, like a child given permission to pick out a single piece of candy at Harris Mercantile.

To be helpful, York said, "I checked with the hotel. They aren't staying there."

Cesar trundled over and stood before the sheriff. Jerked a thumb skyward. "They upstairs. Three doors on the right side. Each got a girl. Even that Preacherman."

"I don't think he's a real preacher, Cesar. Hear anything out of them this morning yet?"

"No, señor."

"Where are their horses? The livery?"

Cesar shook his head. "Hitched out back."

"Any of 'em go out for a ride this morning that you know of?"

"No, señor."

"Pretty sure of that?"

A shoulder went up and down. "I only here since an hour ago, maybe. Maybe they go and get back before I get here. Who can say?"

Cesar did not live on the premises. He and his wife resided in a former hacienda outside town. Some of his girls lived out there, too—not daughters, his . . . girls.

York said, "You don't generally let customers spend the night, do you, Cesar?"

An eloquent shrug. "If they got the dinero, sure they can."

"The Preacherman's party . . . They had the dinero?"

Cesar nodded. "They each got a room up there." Then he frowned and shook a scolding finger. "Killing them one at a time, señor, that could take doing."

"Who said anything about killing them?"

Cesar shrugged again, more matter-of-fact this time. "You go up to arrest them, there be killing, all right."

"Who says I want to arrest them?"

Cesar frowned curiously. "You just asking about them? Really just asking?"

"Really just asking. They're what people in my line of work call suspicious characters."

The proprietor's eyes widened. "They *that*, all right. If you go killing or arresting them, Sheriff, do me a favor? Do it in daylight. Killing at night? Bad for business."

"See what I can do," York said with a chuckle. He arose, tipped his hat, and left Cesar to his work.

Outside, the sun was making its climb, but the late morning remained brisk. York took a left as he exited the cantina and walked around the side of the building, past the exposed wooden staircase up to where soiled doves entertained their patrons. In back, where there was nothing much but a privy and scrubby land that extended into a desert distance, he found three quarter horses hitched up at the leather-glazed hitch rail, two grays and a buckskin.

None of the horses appeared to have been ridden hard of late. No smell of sweat from their coats or any sign of foam, wet or dry. No saddles. Those were probably upstairs with their owners and their hostesses. He supposed one or more of these animals might have been cooled down and brushed after a morning ride. Certainly, none of them seemed tired out.

A sudden hand settled hard on his shoulder, turned him around, away from the horse, and shoved him. After losing his balance, hitting the ground hard, York found himself looking up at Lafe Trammel, the Preacherman's tall, skinny sidekick, who had killed a black cowboy the night before, just inside those adobe walls.

"Let's finish what we started over at the Victory, Sheriff," the lanky Trammel said, fists balled, shoulders hunched, his grin made even more terrible courtesy of the wide space where his two front teeth presumably once had been.

The looming saddle tramp was in his BVD tops and trousers and bare feet, no weapon at his hip. This put

York in a perfect position to kick the idiot in the balls, which was what he did, the hard toe of his boot sinking deep. A howl went up that rivaled any wolf and any moon.

Back on his feet, York appraised his opponent, who was doubled over, even more bowlegged than usual, clutching himself, mouth open, eyes bulging like balloons about to burst.

"Ain't . . . ain't *fair*," Trammel sputtered.

"Neither is this," York said and whipped out his Colt .44 and slapped Trammel across the right cheek with a downward motion, tearing the flesh and leaving a long jagged streak of glistening red behind. The blow dropped the man, who was down on his side on the dusty earth, blubbering like a baby.

Kneeling, York wiped the blood off the barrel of his .44 on Trammel's BVD sleeve and slipped it back into its holster. He was barely to his feet when he realized company was coming.

Moving from around the building came the Preacherman, already in his flapping black coat and hat, accompanied by the pudgy Landrum, who, like the fallen Trammel, was in BVD top and trousers and bare feet, no weapon on his hip.

But Alver Hollis, the Preacherman, surely wore one—a Colt Single Action Army .45, nickel plated, ivory gripped. Legend had it an angel was carved out of either side of those grips, but York hadn't got a close enough look yet to check that out.

Right now the Preacherman's hand hovered over the low-slung handle as he approached as inexorably as a mountain storm.

Perhaps five feet separated York and Hollis—the bucktoothed, piggy sidekick was hanging back another five or more.

The Preacherman, in his deep, mellow voice, asked, "What have you done to my friend, Sheriff?"

He met the man's eyes. "He wanted a fair fight. He came to the wrong place."

Trammel, off to York's right now, was still down in the dust, whimpering, a pile of limbs tossed here and there.

The Preacherman said, " 'An angry person starts fights; a hot-tempered person commits all kinds of sin.' Proverbs twenty-nine, twenty-two."

"I know the one about turning the other cheek, and if your friend gets up, encourage him to do so and see what happens. You fellas sleep in?"

Pausing briefly to process that, Hollis said, "We did. We made a rather late, raucous night of it."

York grinned. "Well, gunning a man down, like your friend here did, that'll take it out of you. So . . . you weren't out riding this morning?"

The Preacherman's hard eyes narrowed. "No. Is there a reason why you're asking? Is that why you're poking around our horses?"

"A man was murdered out on the Bar-O range."

"How tragic. 'No murderer has eternal life abiding in him. John three, fifteen.' "

York turned his grin sideways. "Well, I guess you'd know. This particular murder? Wasn't really your style."

"That so?"

"This was a faked accident. A man supposedly throwed off his horse. You like to take care of your victims in public. Like them to go for their guns first, with plenty of eyes on 'em."

"I have no victims, Sheriff." The shoulders beneath the black suit coat lifted and lowered. "I live in a dangerous world, however, as do you. And at times I must defend myself."

York nodded. "You see, that's why I know you won't draw on me right now. No one to see it but your two gutter ride-alongs. And their kind of testimony might not stand up when the circuit judge comes around."

The Preacherman's smile seemed beneficent. "Why would I want to shoot you, Sheriff? My friend Trammel here . . . *Get up! Get on your feet . . . !* He picked a fight, and he lost. 'For each will have to bear his own load.' Galatians six-five."

"You didn't ask who was killed."

"I don't know many folks around these parts. But do pass along my sympathies to the family of the departed. Afraid I don't read over the dead no more. They'll need someone local."

With a nod, the Preacherman gathered his flock, and they departed, no doubt back to the loft where the ladies of the choir awaited them.

CHAPTER TEN

At 8:00 p.m. on a weeknight, the hotel restaurant was sparsely populated, more waiters than diners—a married couple here, a pair of traveling salesmen there. Folks around town tended to take supper earlier than this, but Caleb York figured the gent who'd invited him here was well aware of that fact.

Grover Prescott, in a tan frock coat with a tan-and-black vest and a tiny black bow tie, was seated alone at a table for four in the far corner of the dining room. The hanging kerosene lamps were turned to a muted glow, lending the dark wood, carved chairs, and linen tablecloths of the chamber an elegance not otherwise found in Trinidad, New Mexico.

Prescott stood and gave the approaching York the kind of smile reserved for close friends, thrusting his hand out for the sheriff to shake, which he did. The railroad man's grip was a tad too tight, showing off some. He was almost as tall as York, a sturdy-looking individual, not quite fat.

York sat, and so did Prescott, who started right in.

"I'm very pleased you agreed to break bread with me, Sheriff," Prescott said. "I was afraid I'd got off on the wrong foot with you at that Citizens Committee meeting the other day."

"Not at all," York said. "I have nothing against a free meal courtesy of the Santa Fe."

"My understanding is that I misjudged you. That you've agreed to cooperate with the town fathers' efforts to make this branchline a reality."

York said, "Let's just say I have an open mind."

Prescott raised a forefinger. "And a realistic one. You're too seasoned a westerner not to know that the future is coming. A man can stand by and wait for the future to come find him, and roll over him, or he can embrace it with open arms and be part of a new day."

Just as at the meeting, everything this slicker said had a practiced sound.

A waiter in black livery arrived to take orders. Prescott read from the menu like a singer from sheet music.

"Let's start with the chicken consommé, followed by the baked salmon à la Chambord. Then filet of veal à la Périgord, with asparagus, new potatoes, and artichokes. For dessert, blancmange. . . . Shall I make that two orders of those selections, Sheriff York?"

"No." His eyes found the waiter's. "Just bring me a beefsteak, rare, thick. Fried potatoes. Coffee. Black."

York's host raised a hand. "Coffee later, perhaps if I can convince you to join me in dessert. For now, waiter, bring us a bottle of your best champagne."

York went along with that. After all, he was the man's guest. A bottle arrived, was opened; glasses were filled.

While they waited for the food, Prescott continued with what was clearly a presentation.

"I understand the Citizens Committee has discussed increasing your pay and providing you with suitable lodgings for a man of your stature."

Somehow York didn't figure Prescott was referring to his six feet one.

"They have," York said. "Contingent on the spur coming through."

Prescott reacted a little to the word *contingent*. Perhaps he'd figured Caleb York would have the vocabulary of a mountain man.

"You may be in a position," Prescott said with a sly smile, "to help make that happen."

York didn't follow up on that—the chicken consommé arrived before he could. Just to have something to do, the sheriff told the waiter to bring him a cup, too.

When the soup was done and the next course had yet to appear, Prescott said, "You may wonder what I mean when I say you could be helpful in making this branchline a reality."

"I don't wonder, really," York said. "You have heard that Willa Cullen and I are friendly, and have been told that I might be able to sway her toward selling you people the right of passage."

Prescott, a trifle surprised, merely nodded.

"But surely you've also heard," York said, "that Miss Cullen is *already* inclined to do business with the Santa Fe. Several members of the Citizens Committee seem well aware that Willa did not support her late daddy in his typically stubborn position."

His expression suddenly grave, Prescott leaned forward. "Let me say, Sheriff, how terrible the Santa Fe finds the loss of George Cullen, one of the true pioneers of this region."

"On the other hand," York said, "his death seems to

clear the path for the railroad and its branchline. One might even call it fortuitous."

Prescott's small plate of baked salmon à la Chambord came. He began to eat, as if that were preferable to actually confirming what York had said.

York continued. "Problem is, with Old Man Cullen murdered? Miss Cullen may not take kindly to any who might have had a hand in it."

A forkful of salmon froze between plate and mouth. "Sir, what are you implying?"

York shrugged and leaned back in his hard, fancy chair. "Not implying a damn thing. Just that those with the best motive for the removal of George Cullen are sitting on the Citizens Committee. Well, most of them, anyway."

Prescott swallowed his bite without taking time to taste it and said, "And *now* what are you implying, Sheriff York?"

"Again, no implication—just fact. You are a suspect in this crime as much as any of our esteemed town fathers. By the way, where were you this morning, between sunup and, say, ten a.m.?"

Prescott pushed away the half-eaten plate of salmon. "I took breakfast here at the hotel around eight. I'm sure you'd have no trouble finding witnesses. At nine I met with Trinidad's new bank president, Harold Turner, to discuss the branchline and how it might benefit his business."

Turner was new in town and had not yet been added to the Citizens Committee, although that seemed inevitable.

York asked, "Have you availed yourself of a horse while visiting our fair community? Bought or rented an animal, or perhaps rented a buggy or buckboard?"

The friendly manner was gone, a coldness taking its place. He knew he was being interrogated.

"Not as of yet," Prescott said. "My business has been confined to town thus far. Eventually, I might be visiting the Bar-O and other, smaller spreads. I have a right of passage to arrange, as you'll recall?"

The main courses arrived, the veal with asparagus, potatoes, and artichokes for Prescott, the rare steak and fried potatoes for York. They ate in silence. The steak was nice and bloody, just the way York liked it.

While he waited for dessert, Prescott said, "May I ask what your intentions are where Miss Cullen is concerned?" Then the railroad man realized his words sounded other than what he'd meant, and added, "Where the branchline is concerned."

The waiter brought York his coffee.

"If you want Miss Cullen's cooperation," the sheriff said after a sip of the stuff, "this murder will have to be solved first. And I aim to do that."

"What if . . . as you speculate . . . the motive has some fool killing Cullen to facilitate the Santa Fe spur?"

York shook his head. "I don't believe the misguided actions of one individual would be enough to make Willa Cullen turn against what she sees as a positive thing for this community, and even her own business."

"You sound sure of that."

"I am. But until that individual is found, the entire Citizens Committee . . . and yourself . . . will seem tarred with the same brush."

Prescott nodded. His coldness was gone, but so was the politician-like manner. "The Santa Fe Railroad would be most grateful to you, sir, should you find the one who did this."

York's eyes tensed. "I wouldn't be looking for a reward."

Rewards, like collecting taxes, were a part of a lawman's due recompense. But this sounded a little too much like a bribe.

Prescott raised a placating palm. "Understood. But we would put our support behind you, Sheriff, and encourage the Citizens Committee to keep you on and make good their promises of better pay and superior housing."

York smiled. "Why do I think there's been some behind-the-scenes discussion among my employers to just put me out of the picture?"

The railroad man shifted in his chair. "Well, you did go around town this morning, questioning each of the town fathers in a murder investigation. Making them feel like . . . suspects."

"That's because they are suspects. So are you."

Prescott only smiled at that. "Since I'm not guilty of anything more than attempted persuasion, that doesn't trouble me, Sheriff. And should your inquiry be successful, I will be in a position to make other recommendations that would be of considerable benefit to you."

"Such as?"

Prescott shrugged. "As Trinidad's population grows, so will its law enforcement requirements. In addition to a county sheriff, there'll be a need for a chief of police and the staff of officers that would go with it, expanding in relation to the population."

"I already have a job."

"Many communities give individuals like yourself multiple positions and multiple paychecks. With my connections, you might also find yourself with deputy U.S. marshal duties in the territory."

York knew Prescott was right—his friends the Earps in

Tombstone had held multiple positions in the manner the railroad man described. It had all worked out well till a certain October afternoon near the O.K. Corral.

The sheriff sat up. "As long as you don't try to influence my investigation in any way, Mr. Prescott, I don't see why we can't be friendly in this."

"Good. Good." A smile became a frown. "One question, Sheriff. What do you know of this Burt O'Malley?"

York shrugged. "He was one of the three men who founded the Bar-O years ago . . . but he did time for a gunfight that went sour. He returned a few days ago, and he and George Cullen seemed to pick up where they'd left off."

Prescott's expression seemed wary. "And O'Malley agreed with Cullen about blocking the spur?"

"Apparently. But I wouldn't put much stake in that."

"Oh?"

York shook his head. "O'Malley wouldn't likely cross Cullen on such a topic right after getting back in the man's good graces. Why? What's your concern?"

Prescott's eyes were tight; his forehead was furrowed. "Just that he might represent Cullen's obstinate point of view where the railroad's concerned. Perhaps as sheriff, you could convince the man to leave. He's a convicted murderer, after all."

Again, York shook his head. "That I won't do for you, Mr. Prescott, however friendly we might be. The man served his time, and, anyway, I don't necessarily think he'll echo Cullen's anti-spur line. But if he does, that's his right."

The forehead smoothed, but the eyes remained tight. "But you will . . . *work* on Miss Cullen?"

"Don't much like the way you put that."

"Just . . . use your influence on her is all I mean to say."

"Don't much like that, either. Don't go ruining our wonderful new friendship, Mr. Prescott."

Another placating palm came up. "I meant no offense."

York's smile lacked humor. "Few who give it do. I will share my opinion, which is favorable to your position, with the young woman. But I won't try to bring her around to my thinking save for some honest talk."

Both palms came up now. "I can ask no more."

York sipped the last of his coffee. "What I *can* do is find a murderer, and maybe that'll put Willa Cullen in a place that's friendly to you and your wishes."

Prescott's dessert arrived—blancmange, cream and sugar thickened with gelatin. "Won't you join me, sir?"

"No thanks," York said, standing. "I'll leave you to it. I'm late for my evening rounds."

And he left the railroad man there to enjoy one sickeningly sweet spoonful after another, with a smile that made York wonder who'd got the best of this meeting.

The evening rounds Caleb York had referred to were generally the duty of Deputy Tulley, whom the sheriff ran into on the boardwalk just down from the hotel. They paused in the shade of the overhang, the street nearby painted blue ivory by a full moon.

The bandy-legged deputy stood with his scattergun cradled in his arms. "Out for a stroll, Sheriff?"

York sighed, eyes traveling. "Just thought with a murderer on the loose, maybe you could stand another pair of eyes tonight."

"Whoever done that deed," Tulley said and spat some tobacco, "has surely crawled in his hidey-hole. He's a sneaky sort, tryin' to blame that killin' on some poor horse that wouldn't throw a man iffen you dug a spur in his flank."

"Does look quiet."

"Quiet as a damn dead dog." Tulley's eyes flicked down the street. "Fairly lively down at the Victory."

"That's where I was headed."

"Need some backup, Sheriff?"

He settled a hand on Tulley's shoulder. "No. You maintain your regular route. You're right. This isn't some mad killer. It's a cold-blooded bastard who picked a blind man for his victim."

Tulley's face wadded itself up. "*Does* sound like somebody needs killin'."

"Does at that."

He left the deputy to walk Main and check the alleys and the residential areas on either side, then headed down to the Victory. Music and laughter and talk spilled out the batwing doors, along with the yellow glow of the kerosene chandeliers within.

After stepping inside, he saw perhaps two dozen cowboys and townsmen having a good time, some bellied up to the bar, others dancing with the satin-wrapped girls. A fair number played poker or faro, though none of the other games of chance were going. Honky-tonk piano cut through a haze of cigar and cigarette smoke. Lovely Rita Filley, the hostess, was threading through, giving customers a smile and sometimes a pat on the shoulder.

Whit Murphy was playing poker at dealer Yancy Cole's table in the company of several of his Bar-O cowpokes, as well as Alver Hollis and his porky sidekick, Landrum. No sign of Trammel. York wandered over and got a look of inquiry from the ruffled-shirt, shuffling-between-hands Cole, who nodded toward an empty chair. York shook his head and instead stood, arms folded, watching, positioned behind Murphy.

As the cards were dealt, the Preacherman—in his usual black, hat and all—said, "Evening, Sheriff."

"Evening," York said, then nodded to the pig-faced Landrum, who said nothing but worked so hard at scowling, it was comical. "Where's your other friend?"

"Lafe Trammel?" Hollis collected his cards with tapering fingers. "Well, that nasty gash you give him this mornin'? Your friend Doc Miller stitched that up some. He took to his bed at the cantina with a bottle of tequila."

"No gal?"

"No gal. Little rest'll do the boy good. 'I will bring health and healing,' Jeremiah, thirty-three, six."

The Preacherman looked at his cards, then glanced up, and York's eyes met his.

York said pleasantly, " 'So I turned my mind . . . to investigate . . . and to understand the stupidity of wickedness.' Believe that's Ecclesiastes, something, something. Tell him I said howdy."

Hollis smiled benevolently. "Glad to, my son."

Whit Murphy tossed in his cards and said, "*Goddamn!*" He cashed in his chips, got back a buck and a half from Cole, and scooted his chair back to wander over to the bar in his bowlegged way, tugging down his high-beamed Carlsbad hat, muttering.

The Bar-O foreman hadn't made it to the bar when York was beside him with a hand on his sleeve. "A word, Whit?"

Murphy shrugged and followed York's lead to a table up front with nobody else nearby.

"Beer?" York asked him.

"Why not?"

The sheriff went over and got a couple of warm beers from bartender Hub Wainwright. He delivered one to Murphy and sat beside him with the other. York sipped some foam off and smiled. Murphy gulped some beer, too.

"Sorry to interrupt your fun," York said.

Murphy grunted, wiping foam from his droopy mustache with his sleeve. "You didn't interrupt no fun at all. I lost pert near five dollars. You think that Preacherman's a cheat or somethin'?"

York had another sip. "Oh, probably. But not likely tonight. He doesn't want to attract any undue attention."

"Dressed like a circuit rider? Ha. But . . . why not?"

"Well, he's here to kill somebody, Whit."

"Hell you say!"

"Sometime before he leaves town, he'll goad somebody into pulling and blow the poor bastard's guts out. That's how he does it."

"Does what?"

"He's a hired killer. If you think he's cheatin' you at the card table, which right now I doubt, you need to do just what you did—throw in your cards and walk away."

Alarm spiked in the foreman's eyes. "You don't think he's here to kill *me*, do you, Sheriff?"

"No. Not unless you got depths I ain't become aware of yet. But I do think he might kill a man who called him a cheat, even if it was just for free."

Murphy's Adam's apple bobbled. "'Preciate the warnin', Sheriff. What, uh, what's it you want with me, anyways?"

York had another swig of the warm brew. "This is the first chance we've had to talk since this morning."

"Since Mr. Cullen got killed, you mean."

"That's right. You've heard that it was a put-up job? Not accidental at all?"

Murphy wiped more beer from his mustache with his sleeve. "I heard. Mr. O'Malley said as much. Miss Cullen knows, too. She's broke up about it but tries not to show it. Ain't seen her cry nary a drop."

"She's a tough girl."

Murphy's humorless half smirk raised one side of the droopy mustache. "She's tougher than most, but it'll still get to her. I ain't ashamed to say I shed a tear or two my own self. He was a fine old fella. Done a lot for me."

"How far back did you go with him?"

"Oh, ten years or more. I was just another cowhand on the spread. He saw somethin' in me and kind of took to me and moved me up. When he made me foreman three years ago or so, I couldn't hardly believe it."

"Tell me about this morning."

Murphy shrugged. "Little to tell. It was just after sunup. He was already on that chestnut he was partial to. Said he was goin' out for a ride, and I said I'd be happy to keep him company. Of course he saw right through that—knew I was just tryin' to worm in and keep him from ridin' off by hisself."

"He do that often? Ride off alone?"

A shrug. "I wouldn't say often. But now and then, the mood would take him. I get it. I get that a man some-times want to be by hisself. A proud man like Mr. Cullen, his sight gone, he sometimes has to feel like a *whole* man, even if he ain't no more."

"And that was the last you saw of him?"

"Last I saw him. Last we spoke."

Murphy sipped beer. So did York.

"Now, Whit. Think carefully. Is there anything else pertinent you can think of?"

"Pert near what?"

"Anything that might be important, considering that we know the old man wasn't really thrown from that chestnut. That somebody murdered him."

Murphy's eyes found the floor. "No. Not really. Only thing, maybe . . . no. No, nothin'."

"Started to sound like something, Whit. What did you see?"

"Nothin' else this mornin'."

"Another time, then? Something suspicious? Come on, Whit. Any small thing could be important."

"Might be nothin'."

"Could be something."

Murphy took a gulp of beer, swallowed it down, and said, "Mr. O'Malley seems like a fine feller."

"Yes, he does. But what *about* Mr. O'Malley?"

"I seen him and Mr. Cullen fighting."

York straightened. "Fighting? Come to blows?"

"No! No. They was on the front porch, talkin'. And it got right heated. They was yellin' at each other. Red in the face and shovin' each other."

"You said they didn't come to blows."

"Well, they didn't! Shovin' ain't blows. Nothin' hard enough to knock one or the t'other down. But they was riled, very damn riled."

"What was it about?"

Murphy pawed the air. "Weren't my business. I felt kind of . . . embarrassed like. I don't think they seen me. I was on my way back to the bunkhouse, and I just got there all the faster."

"But you saw enough to tell that they were arguing. Heatedly."

"I did."

"Was Willa around?"

"No, sir. She would've been to bed by then. Was midnight or thereabouts."

"What were you doing up that late, Whit?"

"Headin' out to the privy. So I was a good distance from the porch at the time. Didn't hear a word, just the sound of an argument. Couldn't make out nothin' . . . but wasn't tryin' to."

York nodded. "You mention this to anybody? Willa maybe?"

Murphy's eyes flared. "No, sir! And I ain't about to say nothin' to that O'Malley feller, neither."

"No?"

"No! What if he's a murderer?"

York couldn't argue with that. He dug a half eagle out of his pocket and tossed it to Murphy.

"Have another go at the cards," York said, "on me. Just don't accuse that Preacherman of cheating."

"Even if he is?"

"Especially if he is."

Murphy ambled over there, half a beer in hand, and filled the seat he'd vacated not long ago.

York was just sitting there, mulling the conversation with Murphy, when Rita settled in next to him. She was wearing a blue-and-black satin number that cupped her full breasts lovingly; her dark hair was up in a mass of curls; her full lips were rouged red, her cheeks touched red, too.

"Fascinating character to talk to?" she asked. "Whit Murphy?"

"He knows a thing or two."

"About this murder of yours?"

York frowned at her. "It's all over town, is it?"

"You surprised? You went around questioning every city father this morning." She shook her head, and the curls bounced; so did her bosom, a little. "Terrible thing. That George Cullen was the bedrock of this community."

"He didn't see it that way. He was all about the Bar-O. If the old man'd had the vision his daughter *has*, then maybe—"

Big brown eyes got bigger. "The daughter, huh? You and Willa kiss and make up, did you?"

"Not really."

That made Rita smile. She and York had gotten friendly in recent months. He'd become quite familiar with her fancy remodeled quarters upstairs.

She flicked the tin star on his chest. "Why don't you take that off and have a little fun?"

"I don't cotton to the company."

"I hope you mean the Preacherman, and not yours truly." She shrugged. "Preacherman's been behaving himself."

"He'll kill somebody before he's through. Right at that table."

"You really think so?"

"He's a hired gun, Rita, with a built-in cover story. Please keep that pretty head of yours out of the line of fire when he's around."

She frowned. "You think he killed George Cullen?"

"No. Not his style."

"So we have two killers in town."

"No," York said. He held up three fingers.

"Who's the other one . . . ? Oh. You."

He didn't say anything. He didn't have to.

"Would you like to come upstairs, Caleb?"

Very much, he would have liked to come upstairs. But somehow, right now, with Willa back in his life . . . for how long, and in what way, he couldn't say . . . he was better off letting Rita down easy.

"Honey," he said, "I *am* working. Maybe tomorrow."

"I'll be here," she said.

CHAPTER ELEVEN

Half a mile out of town, the rough-hewn sign by the roadside said TRINIDAD CEMETERY, but locals called it Boot Hill, inaccurate though that might be for such a flat, scrubby patch of dusty earth overseen by a single stubborn mesquite tree and disrupted by frequent wooden crosses and occasional tombstones. In the distance, the steep cliffs of buttes, with grooves carved vertically by erosion, made long, sorrowful faces as citizens from the nearby town and its environs made their way in buggies and on horseback.

The cemetery's residents lay close enough together to make graveside services awkward: when a sizable crowd like this morning's was in attendance, mourners had no choice but to gather in lanes between the previously buried. The morning was cold but still, no wind stirring at all, as if the earth were as dead as the man this group of several hundred in Sunday best was seeing off.

Caleb York had attended several such services at Boot Hill, but never one so well attended by such a variety of citizens. All the Citizens Committee members, standing together, with wives and families—but for the widowers and bachelors—were along one side of the grave. Other respectable townsfolk had assembled to the rear on that same side, while opposite were cowhands from the Bar-O— Whit Murphy right in front—and other spreads, including rival ranchers; they too were in attire reserved for church, weddings and, of course, funerals. Hats were respectfully in hand.

Toward the back, in apparel considerably less gaudy than their working clothes, were Rita Filley, her girls, and the bartending staff. Now and then the young women would receive sharp, reproving glances from wives, while the husbands wouldn't look in that direction at all. The contingent from the Victory paid no heed to either slight.

At the foot of the grave, in which was Undertaker Perkins's finest mahogany, brass-fitted casket, stood Willa Cullen, between Burt O'Malley and a tall, distinguished-looking gentleman in his fifties, whom York did not know. The well-barbered, white-haired, white-mustached stranger looked like money in his double-breasted, gray, trimmed-black newmarket coat, double-breasted lighter gray waistcoat, and darker gray trousers, white top hat in hand.

Furthermore, the gent had his arm through Willa's, who was in a long-sleeved silk mourning dress under a matching black parasol. A relative, perhaps? York couldn't recall her mentioning anyone who might fit the bill.

Reading words over the deceased, lanky, mutton-chopped Reverend Caldwell from Missionary Baptist was standing just to one side of the temporary wooden marker, which would be replaced by a tombstone, expected within the month from Denver by way of Las Vegas. Toward the rear, under the mesquite, like a vulture and a couple of crows who'd fallen from it, lurked the undertaker in his black stovepipe hat with two Mexican grave diggers with shovels ready to fill in the hole when respects had been paid.

"Blessed are those who mourn," the reverend was saying, reading from the Good Book, "for they will be comforted."

The Scripture reading served only to remind York of one person not in attendance: the Preacherman. But then, Alver Hollis had never met George Cullen . . . had he?

Moving through the crowd as inconspicuously as possible, York made his way to Willa. He came up behind the girl and slipped between her and O'Malley, giving the man a nod. She glanced up at York and smiled just a little. He would have liked to hold her hand, but she was clutching that parasol, and, anyway, things hadn't entirely warmed up between them.

So he settled on just touching her shoulder briefly and giving it a gentle squeeze.

He recalled what Whit Murphy had said last evening at the Victory—she was not crying and showed no signs of having been. No redness, no watery setting for the dark blue eyes. Just a lovely, stoic expression.

Glancing around at the attendees, his gaze drifting across the assembled Citizens Committee, York couldn't help but think how hypocritical some of them were, mourning—or pretending to—the death of the man who had stood in the way of their potential prosperity. As his eyes took their grim inventory, he noticed how glum Rita's expression was, her own eyes taking inventory, as well, noting his presence at Willa's side.

When the service was over, and Willa had tossed in a black-lace-gloved handful of dirt, she turned slowly to look around at the crowd and announce strongly, "We'll be serving lunch at the Bar-O. I hope you all will be able to join us and share happy memories of my father."

This was no surprise—an after-funeral meal from the grieving family was quite common, particularly among those better off. So was good-natured gossip and yarn spinning about the departed.

As the crowd dispersed, Willa turned to York and gestured to the distinguished figure at her side.

"Caleb York," she said, "Raymond L. Parker."

Thinking, *I should have known*, York held out a hand and received a firm, warm handshake in return. This was the third partner in the original Bar-O, the one who had sold out to make his fortune elsewhere some years ago.

And make it Parker had, with hotels and banking interests in both Denver and Kansas City.

"Mr. Parker," York said, "despite the circumstances, it's good to finally meet you."

The white-mustached face gave the sheriff as wide a smile as the occasion dared.

Parker said, "George spoke most highly of you, son. And, of course, your storied reputation precedes you."

"The former honors me," York said, "but you'd be wise to ignore the latter."

They began to walk for the waiting buggy, O'Malley taking Willa's arm, while York and Parker followed, chatting.

York said, "I'm surprised you were able to get here so quickly, sir."

"Train, stagecoach, and finally a Morgan horse I bought out at the Brentwood Junction crossroads. Cost a pretty penny. But I'd have made the journey on foot, if needs must."

"Staying at the Bar-O?"

"Uh, no. In town. At the hotel."

"That's where I room. Perhaps we can dine in the restaurant there this evening."

Something tightened around Parker's eyes, which York couldn't read. "I'd like that, son, but not this evening. Afraid I have business to attend to. Breakfast tomorrow, perhaps? The café?"

"Certainly."

Business? What business?

Soon the buggy—O'Malley at the reins and Willa between him and Parker—swung out to the right, in the direction of the Bar-O, falling in with the other buggies, buckboards, and horseback riders on their way to the luncheon.

York was about to mount his black-maned, dappled gray gelding when he realized Rita was at his side.

She was in a black dress trimmed with white, what sometimes was called half mourning, referring to a stage of grief as shown by a widow. Like Willa, Rita had a parasol, though hers was white. Still, seeing the two women dressed so similarly gave York a sudden realization of how much alike they were physically, and how young they both were. The major difference, of course, was Willa's Nordic coloring and Rita's half-Latin heritage.

Parasol resting on her shoulder, she aimed her big brown eyes up at him and asked, "So was he here, do you think?"

"Who?"

"The one who killed him."

York drew in a breath, let it out slow. "Probably."

"A face in this crowd give anything away?"

Just you, he thought, *when you saw me standing beside Willa.*

"No," he said. "Guilt is good at pretending to be sorrow."

An eyebrow went up. "*Someone* wasn't here this morning. Of course, he's not a citizen."

"The Preacherman, you mean? And his toadies?"

She nodded. "Have you really ruled him out?"

"Not entirely. There's a reason why his usual method wouldn't have worked in this case."

"What's that?"

"You can't goad a blind man into pulling on you."

She laughed a little. "I suppose you're right. Old Man Cullen didn't wear a gun on his hip, but he often had a rifle in hand. That might have been enough to give the Preacherman his out."

York shook his head. "Not likely. Not with me as sheriff. I'd have gone after him and brought him back slung over a saddle."

"You mean, you'd just kill him?"

He grinned at her. "I didn't say that. Probably I'd just have . . . goaded him into going for it."

She smiled back at him, something impish in it. "You're very bad for a good man, Caleb York."

"Or good for a bad man," he said with a shrug. "You have to fight evil with evil's means. . . . Listen, I'm glad you stopped me. I wanted to talk to you. And I figure you won't be at the luncheon."

She paused, possibly trying to decide whether or not to take offense. Then the impish smile returned, but with something sad in it now.

"You're right, Caleb," she said. "My girls and I and Hub and the rest of the staff, we need to get back and open up the Victory. Otherwise, I'm *sure* we'd be welcome at the Bar-O."

Her sarcasm chastised him.

He said, "I might've mispoken. Miss Cullen is a pretty open-minded gal."

Rita's smirk was almost a kiss. "Not where I'm concerned, I'm afraid. I think she sees me as the competition. Isn't that silly? Isn't that just utter foolishness?"

He didn't know what to say to that, so he said, "Look, uh, about that poker tourney of yours tomorrow night."

Her eyebrows went up. "What about it? You're signed on. You have a seat at one of the tables."

"That's what I wanted to talk to you about. How many tables will there be?"

She frowned, wondering what this was about. "Just three."

"Can you make sure I'm seated at the same table as Alver Hollis? And put his two cronies there, too."

Half a smile joined her frown. "You want to share a table with the Preacherman? Why? Do you need to get some religion?"

"The words that real preacher spoke over George Cullen's grave are all the religious teaching I need. I just want to make sure, when that tourney starts, that I'm sitting with Hollis and company. Can you handle that?"

She nodded, but her eyes were narrow. "You're not going to spoil my big event, are you?"

"Not unless the Preacherman already has that in mind. He's said specifically he's in town for the big game and will leave shortly thereafter. And I'm convinced he's in town to kill somebody."

She was nodding. "So if he hasn't earned his gunman's pay by the time the game starts, then . . ."

"Someone in that game is set to die."

All but a few of the mourners had made their exit, a

handful taking the opportunity to have some time at this or that grave of a family member or friend. Undertaker Perkins and his Mexican boys were waiting impatiently beneath the mesquite for the cemetery to clear.

York was up on his gelding, but Rita was still alongside, a hand on the animal's rump, her pretty, wide-eyed face tilted toward the sheriff.

"I can give you the list of players," she said. "That might give you an idea of who the Preacherman intends to send to their reward."

"I was hoping I might ask for that," he said, damn near grinning. "That could be a big help."

"I'll make a copy."

He reined up the animal. "I'll send Tulley down to pick it up. Much obliged to you, ma'am."

Her smile showed small, perfect teeth. "Call me 'ma'am' again and I'll slap that horse on the rump and send you for a good damn ride."

He chuckled and headed out, the gelding going nice and easy.

At the Bar-O, just inside and under the log arch bearing the ranch's brand, a dozen picnic tables borrowed from the church had been set up in the front yard, the main ranch house looking on in the background.

Also looming was the cookhouse, with its hand pump and tin basin–lined bench under an awning-shaded porch; smoke twirled out of the cookhouse chimney like a lazy lariat.

But there was nothing lazy about what went on within the log building, where Harmon, the plump, white-bearded Bar-O cook—who'd been at it since sunup—and several helpers were turning out fried chicken, dumplings, potato salad, and apple pie. Coffee and milk were flowing, too. The seated guests were served by Bar-O cowhands still in their Sunday-style finery, and the air was filled with stories about George Cullen, some amusing, some hair raising, but clearly the residue of a life lived large.

York sat with O'Malley beside him and Parker across the way. Willa had disappeared somewhere, but a seat next to the guest from Denver was reserved for her. The bachelor mayor was just down from them, regaling newspaperman Penniman—his wife and two children nearby—with examples of how generous the late Bar-O owner had been with the town of Trinidad, such as when he had donated the money needed to build Missionary Baptist Church. Doc Miller was down there eating chicken and keeping to himself, ignoring the foofaraw.

Perhaps it was just the mayor dominating the talk that made it so, but York found it interesting and a little unsettling that he hadn't heard O'Malley and Parker exchange as much as a word. These two old friends, reunited after so many years, seemed to have nothing to say to each other.

Was there something significant about Parker staying at the hotel and not here at the ranch? Where O'Malley was already bunking down?

Suddenly heads were turning, and York swung in that direction himself. There, on the ranch-house porch, stood Willa Cullen, in her familiar red-and-black plaid shirt and denim pants, all that yellow hair braided up, the mourning attire already tucked away.

With all those eyes on her, she merely smiled, chin up a little, and called out, "I'm so pleased you could join us here at the Bar-O! This is exactly the kind of celebration my father would've relished!"

Then she came over to the head picnic table and took her seat next to Raymond Parker, who was looking at her with quiet amusement. York was doing the same.

"What?" she asked, glancing up at them from the big dish of potato salad, a heaping spoonful of which she was transferring to her plate.

"People will talk," York said, mischief in his voice.

Her chin came up even more. "Let them. They need to know that the Bar-O is up and running, and doing just fine."

"And," Parker said, "you want them to know who's in charge."

Actually, York thought, *who's* still *in charge*.

"If they take me for some helpless young thing," she said, "I'll spend all my time fighting off those who want to ride roughshod over me."

"Heaven help them," York said.

She blushed but was smiling.

O'Malley wasn't smiling. If anything, he seemed on the doleful side.

By mid-afternoon, most everybody had collected their rides and gone back off to town. The sporadic caravan of buggies, buckboards, and horses raised a small dust storm down the dirt road.

Parker and Willa were still at their table, talking. O'Malley had moved to the porch, where he sat on a rough-hewn chair probably hammered together by their late host, and puffed away on a cigar.

Another such chair was next to the man, and York took it.

"Mind if I interrupt the festivities," York said, "to ask a few lawman type of questions?"

"I'd say the festivities are pretty well worn down already," the big man said, with that easy half smile of his. "And if you have a job to do, by all means do it."

York nodded around them. "Right here on this porch, night before things went tragic, you were seen arguin' with the old man. Word is it got right heated."

"Is that what the word is?"

"It is."

The dark blue eyes fixed on York unblinkingly. "Who told you that? I don't remember anybody bein' around."

"So you don't deny the two of you argued?"

The intense eyes stayed right on York. "Answer my question first, Sheriff. Who told you I got into it with ol' George?"

"Just one of the cowpokes who made a run out to the privy and happened to hear."

"What did they happen to hear?"

"Not much. Didn't want to intrude but couldn't help noticin', what with voices raised and all. What *might* they have heard if they hadn't been so mindful of their manners?"

The dark blue eyes turned away, looked out into the afternoon, where the cleanup of the luncheon was under way. "I wanted to buy back in."

"Earlier he offered you one of the smaller spreads, to be your own. For the money he'd put aside for you."

O'Malley was nodding. "And that was generous. And I am still considerin' that. But I felt . . . and this is what made the old boy get touchy . . . that he shouldn't leave the Bar-O in the hands of some little snip of a gal."

"I'd imagine he said Willa wasn't just 'some little snip.' That she was his blood and that he'd raised her to it, and that she was damn near born in a saddle. Words to that effect."

"Words to that effect."

York slapped his thigh. "So. Who shoved who?"

O'Malley sat forward in his chair. "Nobody shoved nobody. Maybe a finger got stuck in a chest here and there. I don't fight with old blind men, particular old blind men that I love. You got that, Caleb York? I *loved* that old man."

O'Malley's finger was raised at York's chest level, as if about to thump again. The big man realized as much and withdrew it.

O'Malley swallowed thickly, then said, "All I want to do, Sheriff, is help in this investigation of yours. Tell me, please, is there anything I can do?"

York shrugged. "Just stay on here at the ranch and keep an eye on Willa."

"I can do that."

"But can you not pressure her in any way—for or against—concerning how she should go where this spur is concerned? And if you see anybody doing that, again *whichever* side, advise 'em politely to back off."

"How politely?"

York grinned. "Stoppin' short of getting yourself sent back to the hoosegow."

O'Malley grinned back. "I can handle that, Sheriff."

York got up, then swiveled back. "Oh, one last thing . . ."

"Yeah?"

"Everything okay between you and Parker? Seems a mite . . . stiff, you ask me."

O'Malley sighed. "I was never that thick with Raymond. It was always George I was close to. We always rubbed each other wrong, Parker and me. I was probably part of why he went off on his own all them years ago."

"He should thank you, as well as he's done."

O'Malley chuckled. "You're right, Sheriff. You are so very right. But I won't waste time waitin' for a check to arrive."

Before leaving, York knocked on the front door, and on the second knock, Willa answered.

"Caleb," she said.

"Willa," he said.

Awkward silence.

Then from Willa: "Thank you for coming."

That was the kind of ridiculous thing people said to each other in such circumstances. As if he would under any conditions not attend the funeral of the great man who was her father. Or not stand at her side at that event.

"I wanted to know," he said, "if there was anything I could do."

Another ridiculous remark in such a situation.

"There is something," she said. She stuck her head out the door, noticed down the porch O'Malley sitting and smoking, and curled a finger at York to come inside.

They sat together on the hearth, the warmth of a small crackling fire at their backs. She found his hand. It was warm, too.

"Forgive me for asking," she said. "I know I probably don't really *need* to, but . . ."

"I'll find the one who did it, Willa. Make no mistake of that."

Neither was looking at the other.

"I know," she said. "I know you will, and I know that you are a genuine detective, if nothing else. But you're also . . . You are a killer of men, Caleb York. No doubt of that."

"No doubt."

"I want your promise that you will not just find who-

ever did this terrible thing, but that you will kill that person, or persons. Even if you have to take off your badge
to do it."

"You have my word." He was looking at her now,
though her eyes were aimed straight ahead. "Your father's murderer will pay the ultimate price. Not a rope.
But my gun."

Now she looked at him.

She squeezed his hand very hard. Then she kissed him
the same way. The fire at their backs was hot, but not
that hot.

Swallowing for breath, York placed a finger on her
ripe lips. "You must promise me something now."

"Anything."

"You must follow your heart and your mind in this
matter. You have people all around you jockeying to 'help'
you, all with their own self-interests at the root. You will
have all the city fathers, from the mayor on down, trying
to manipulate you. Even those who mean well, like Whit
and your uncle Burt, see things from their own perch.
This railroad agent, Prescott, will wave money in your
face that would tempt a saint. But hold fast to whatever
you think is best."

Now she was looking at him, while he stared straight
ahead.

She said, "You told me you agree that selling the right
of passage makes sense."

He nodded. "That's my opinion. My self-interest is
that I'll get a raise and a house out of it, and I'll have a
town growing around me that will enhance my financial
position. My position, period. Any credence you give to
my views, keep that in mind."

Her sigh was punctuated by crackling flames. "Until

somebody killed Daddy over it, I intended to sell. Now . . .
I find myself wanting to respect his views."

"No."

"No?"

"He's gone. And when he was here, he was of another
time, almost of another place. The future's upon us, and
there's no escaping it. You must make this decision yourself. All this advice will be whirling around your head,
but it all boils down to selling a right-of-way to the railroad or, frankly, selling the Bar-O entirely."

"Two simple courses of action."

"Two simple courses of action . . . Getting a little
warm, don't you think?"

They shared grins and stood up, the backs of their
clothing hot enough to smoke.

Facing the fire now, Willa at his side, York said, "You
could use a portrait of your papa over the mantel here. I
know a good artist in Dodge City. Are there any photo-
graphs of the old boy he might work from?"

She nodded. "Yes. And I'd love that."

"Round me your favorite tintypes of your papa, and
I'll take care of it. My treat." His eyes moved to either
side of the mantel. "Those rifles are something to see."

On the left was a 50-70 Gov't Sharps rifle, and on the
right a Winchester Model 1866, each cradled in mortar-
mounted, upturned deer-hoof gun racks.

She said, "Papa came west with a horse and that
Sharps rifle. Buffalo hunting laid the groundwork for
what became the Bar-O. Our distinguished guest from
Denver was at his side through all of it."

Raymond Parker had hidden depths.

"Are they loaded?" York asked.

"Oh, my, yes. To me and everybody else, they were

decoration. For Papa, they were protection. You never knew when another Indian uprising was on the horizon."

They both laughed a little at that; then she walked him out, hand in hand until they reached the porch, when her fingers slipped away. Apparently, she wasn't ready to advertise her feelings for him, with O'Malley on the porch and the cook staff and cowboys cleaning up the tables and disassembling them to be stacked in a buckboard for return to Missionary Baptist.

She did walk him to the dappled gelding at a hitch post near the barn.

He was about to get up onto the saddle when she said, very softly, "Do you think I'm terrible?"

He thought she was wonderful.

"No," he said.

"I mean . . . asking you to kill somebody in cold blood."

"There'll be nothing cold about it." He swung up onto the horse, then looked down at her with the faintest of smiles. "And it won't be murder, exactly. The one I kill will have his fair chance. He'll go for his gun before I do mine. I'll arrange that."

That much he had in common with the Preacherman.

He waved as he rode out, and she waved back and smiled. Still no sign of tears.

CHAPTER TWELVE

When Caleb York got to the café just before eight the next morning, it took him a couple of blinks to recognize Raymond Parker.

The distinguished city clothes were gone, and in their stead were a dark gray sateen shirt with arm garters and a cowhide vest, a yellow knotted bandana at the throat and, resting on the table beside him, an uncreased broad-brimmed hat, which took the place of the cemetery's white stovepipe.

Suddenly York could see the frontiersman who lived within the big-city businessman, the onetime partner of George Cullen who'd helped carve out the Bar-O. Parker had mentioned that he'd bought a horse at Brentwood Junction and ridden into Trinidad . . . and the man wouldn't have done that dressed in a newmarket coat, a double-breasted waistcoat, and fancy trousers.

A smile blossomed under the well-trimmed white mustache, and the tall figure at the small table by the window in the unpretentious café got to his feet and offered his hand. Again, the sheriff clasped hands with the visitor, and confident firmness sent its message to both.

York, in his usual black, removed his hat and hung it on a hook by the door nearby. He sat across from the businessman, a white enamel coffeepot and two matching cups already waiting. The café, as usual, was bustling. They served a good breakfast at about half the price of the hotel, and as long as you didn't prefer linen to checkered tablecloths, this was your place.

"How clear is your morning, Sheriff York?" Parker's voice was a husky mid-range growl as firm and confident as that handshake.

"Clear enough," York said with a shrug.

"Good. There's some business we need to attend to later."

Business again. What business does a man with holdings in Denver and Kansas City have in Trinidad, New Mexico?

A waiter in an apron came over and got their order— griddle cakes for Parker, eggs and bacon and grits for York.

As they waited, Parker offered York a tailor-made cigarette from a silver case, a hint that the Denverite was no longer a man who spent much time in the saddle. York refused with a smile, and Parker lit up.

"We met on a buffalo hunt, George Cullen and I," Parker said, sighing smoke, as if he were answering a question York hadn't asked. "It was the start of both our fortunes, but looking back, I sometimes wonder. Was it our original sin?"

"Not many buffalo left," York said as he poured himself coffee. Parker already had some.

"Less than a hundred of the animals, I hear. We hunted them for their skins and left the rest of the beasts behind to rot." He shook his head. "Such easy pickings—kill one of the animals and the rest would gather around. Kill one, kill a whole herd."

"Why was the meat left to waste?"

Parker let out more smoke, shrugged, his expression somber. "The government was paying us. They wanted to get rid of the food source for those poor damn Indians. That was something we didn't think about at the time. And by the time it ever did occur to us, we'd kind of built up a grudge against the red man. Encounter a few hostiles and you aren't filled with much sympathy. Anyway, we were young bucks and sought adventure and profit, and I won't lie to you and say I've spent much time feeling guilty about it. Men get caught up in a life and they live it, and then, one day, it's over. As it was for George Cullen."

York cocked his head. "I knew him only in his later years, but he was as honest and brave an individual as I have ever met."

"Here's to George Cullen," Parker said.

They toasted coffee cups.

Their breakfasts came, and they ate, with intermittent conversation limited to mostly how good the grub was and the weather and such like.

"So here we are," Parker said, "all these years later, and the red natives are consigned to reservations and the scrap heap of history, and we are left to try to build something on what we did, whether it was right or wrong."

"Civilization, you mean."

"Civilization, exactly. If we are going to push out a whole goddamned people and take their place, don't we have a responsibility to at least make the best of it? If we wind up bigger savages, how can we justify it . . . ? These griddle cakes are first rate."

"You should try the grits."

He shuddered. "Must be a Southern cook back there."

"I'm trying to read between the lines, Mr. Parker, and I'm thinking you believe your old partner was wrong to buck the railroad."

"Oh, he was wrong, all right." Parker grunted something like a laugh. "He could have a hard head, George Cullen. It's a good thing his daughter has a more level one. My understanding is she's in favor of the branchline."

"She is, and she isn't."

Parker frowned, pushing aside a plate where one last bite of griddle cake swam alone in syrup. "Mind explaining that?"

"She was for the spur. Then, after somebody killed her daddy over it, she didn't care to give the murderer his way. Or, I should say, right-of-way."

"Ah. And where do *you* stand?"

York flipped a hand. "Nominally, I'm with the branchline contingent. They've promised me a raise and a house and general prosperity, to go along with Trinidad turnin' into another Las Vegas."

Parker's eyes narrowed; those eyebrows were as pure white as the mustache. "Let's back up to that word 'nominally.'"

York shrugged. "I like Willa. I'll support her in whichever way she goes in this. If I lose this job, I have another waiting."

"In San Diego. With the Pinkertons. For excellent pay."

"That's right."

The white eyebrows lifted. "Kind of hard to 'like' a gal from that distance."

"I'm kind of taking it a day at a time. We've had a bump or two in the road, Willa and me."

"Such as you killing her fiancé?"

"You heard about that? Yeah." York poured himself more coffee. "But into each life a little rain must fall. Anyway, my job right now is to find her father's killer."

"Getting anywhere?"

"No shortage of suspects when the victim was standin' in the way of a whole town getting rich."

Parker let out a lazy wreath of cigarette smoke. "Any particular suspect getting your attention?"

"Maybe one. What can you tell me about your other old partner? Burt O'Malley?"

Parker's expression shifted, as if his bellyful of griddle cakes was suddenly giving him indigestion. "I did not share George Cullen's enthusiasm for that man."

York sipped coffee. "He seems decent enough. Affable. Concerned about Willa. Broke up about the old man. All his reactions are the right ones."

"And that bothers you some? Because maybe they seem a little *too* right?"

"Not sure. When George Cullen was alive, O'Malley sided with him against the spur. Now he's talkin' otherwise. And he's encouraging Willa to let him buy into the Bar-O with the money her daddy put away for him during his imprisonment. That George Cullen would do such a generous thing—for a partner who killed a man—says something good about both of them . . . doesn't it?"

Parker didn't answer right away. He dropped his spent cigarette to the floor and ground it out with his boot heel.

Then he said, "Ever wonder why I ceased being a part

of the Bar-O, despite the depth of friendship between George Cullen and myself?"

"I have at that," York admitted. "But what business is it of mine?"

"In a murder investigation," Parker said, "possibly very much your business. That man O'Malley killed . . . Have you heard the story? His version of the story?"

York said he had. That a rich man's son had forced himself on a woman both he and O'Malley loved. That the ruined woman had hanged herself the night before she and O'Malley were to be wed.

Parker gave up an elaborate shrug. "It may have happened that way. But at the trial there were those who said O'Malley's woman and the rich boy were together because they wanted to be. That she intended to throw Burt over, and her suicide may have been something else. Something Burt himself did."

Parker let York think about that for a while.

York did, then said, "And you thought his version of what happened was a lie."

It wasn't exactly a question.

Another, more casual shrug came from Parker. "I didn't know then, and I don't know now. But one thing I *do* know—Burt O'Malley was damn well aware that this Leon Packett character who he shot did *not* have a gun on him. Even if it was in a way justified, and Burt's story about the tragedy that befell his loyal bride-to-be was not of his own invention, it was *still* murder. Cold blooded and well considered."

"George Cullen believed him."

"He did. And when George told me he wanted us to bank O'Malley's share of Bar-O earnings during the man's incarceration, I wanted none of it. I gave George the opportunity to buy me out. I'd been thinking about it a long time, anyway."

"Oh?"

Parker nodded. "O'Malley always struck me as one of those smilers who slapped you on the back till it was time to slide a blade in. Anyway, I wanted a different kind of life—the big-city variety. You get older, and the dust and manure and the long damn days on a ranch can get to you. Plus, the future was calling. And I have no regrets to this day, leaving it all behind."

York had only eaten half of his breakfast; what was left was cold, and he pushed the plate away. "You have only your suspicions."

He nodded. "Only my suspicions. Or . . . *mostly* only my suspicions."

"What else, then?"

Parker leaned in. "When he was released from prison, Burt O'Malley first came to see me—not to George Cullen, but to *me*. We had never really had a falling-out, O'Malley and myself, and I don't suppose he even knew the role he'd played in my decision to sell out my interests in the Bar-O. So it wasn't an unnatural thing, coming to see me . . . for a loan."

"That's why he came to you? A loan?"

Another nod. "Burt told me that he felt bad for George, now a blind old man with no sons to carry on. You and I know that Willa is as strong as any son, but Burt had no way of knowing that, at least not till I told him. And plenty of men would dismiss a daughter's claim, anyway. What he wanted was a loan to put with the money George had put away for him . . . so that he could buy into the Bar-O to such a degree that when George Cullen passed, the ranch would be mostly his."

"You turned O'Malley down."

"Not at first. I did give it some thought. A week went by, and Burt came around and told me about the proposed spur and the windfall it would represent to the Bar-O. He offered to cut me in for twenty percent of his share of the Bar-O if I would just back him in his play. That's how he put it—his play."

"Nothing illegal about any of that."

"No. But I sent him packing. And, obviously, he returned to the Bar-O, anyway, with the money that had been put away for him, and proceeded to cozy up to the old man and the daughter."

York was frowning. "How did a jailbird come to know of that branchline?"

"That Prescott character looked him up. Wouldn't be surprised if the Santa Fe Ring didn't pull some strings to get O'Malley sprung from the Kansas State Pen early."

York thought about that.

Then he asked, "You think O'Malley's capable of killing Cullen?"

"I do," came the unhesitating answer. "But 'capable' doesn't mean he did it. In a way, without my backing, it doesn't make sense for him to have done so. After all, he wasn't able to buy into the Bar-O."

"I think he might be able to buy in, at that."

"How so?"

York leaned forward. "Well, for one thing, maybe Prescott and the Santa Fe were willing to back him. And he's also got himself very much on Willa's good side now. There had been talk of him buying one of the smaller spreads that the Bar-O recently swallowed up. But O'Malley told her he'd much prefer to buy into the Bar-O itself."

"Do you think he could manipulate her into that?"

"Not with me around." York's own quick remark made something stir in the back of his brain. Then he said, "You said we had business. What business is that?"

"We finished here?"

"Sure."

Parker rose, tossed a half eagle on the table to cover generously the breakfasts and a tip, and they headed out onto the boardwalk.

As if Parker were the one who lived here, York followed him down and across the street. At first York thought they were headed to the newspaper, but the destination turned out to be next door to the *Enterprise*— the law office of Arlen Curtis.

York followed Parker into the big square single room. No secretary awaited, and only a few chairs at right and left served as a reception area. Much of the central space was taken up by a massive, heavy oaken table, which Curtis—a broad-shouldered, dark-bearded fellow in black who resembled General Grant—used for a desk.

The tabletop's clutter included stacks of papers, a few thick legal tomes, ink bottles, pens in a drinking glass, and a lion's-head press for applying seals. The walls were papered an undecorative faint yellow, and the back one bore several roll-down maps and a pigeonhole rack of papers and office supplies, with more legal books stacked on top. Below the rack a fat safe squatted like an eavesdropper.

Curtis stood, and a smile peeked out of the thicket of dark beard. "Right on time, gentlemen," he said.

York blinked. *Right on time?*

Two client chairs were waiting. Both Parker and York shook hands with Curtis; then everyone took their seats. The lawyer flipped through several pages of a legal document, found what he was looking for, then looked up pleasantly at his visitors.

"With your permission," the lawyer said, "I believe we can do without certain formalities."

"We can?" York asked.

Curtis nodded. "There is only one bequest, Sheriff York, and it concerns you."

"Bequest? What is this? The reading of a will?"

Curtis flicked another smile. "Well, of course. Hasn't Mr. Parker made that clear?"

"He has not," York said, giving the businessman a sharp sideways look.

"Mr. Curtis," Parker said, sitting forward, "the sheriff and I had to discuss a few things first, which we have done. I didn't think the purpose of *this* meeting needed to be one of them. We were in a public place, after all."

York, frowning, said, "We were talking murder over breakfast, and that didn't seem to be a concern! What the hell is going on here?"

Thick black eyebrows rose as the lawyer fixed his gaze on the sheriff. "Why, the reading of George Oliver Cullen's last will and testament, of course. Mr. Parker here is the executor, and you, Mr. York, are the sole beneficiary."

York sat forward on his hard chair. "Well, that's absurd. Why would I be the beneficiary of anything? Why isn't Cullen's daughter, Willa, here? Surely, she inherits everything!"

Curtis raised a calming hand. "Sheriff York, if you will

think back . . . during the difficulties with your late pre-decessor, Sheriff Harry Gauge, Mr. Cullen transferred all his holdings to his daughter. She does not need to inherit the Bar-O and all its assets, because she *already* owns them."

York squinted at the lawyer. "Oh-kay . . . Then why . . . ?"

The lawyer flipped a page of the legal document. "There is a parcel of land, actually several adjacent parcels, that Mr. Cullen has left to you. This property is separate from the Bar-O and its holdings."

Still squinting, as if hoping to bring the lawyer into focus, York said numbly, "He left me some land."

"Yes. If you will forgive my speaking out of school, the late Mr. Cullen indicated that he held you in high regard, sir, and that he had hopes that you and his daughter would, well . . . I believe you know what those hopes were. Mr. Cullen wanted to encourage you to maintain residence in this part of the world. And this bequest was his way of trying to accomplish that."

York leaned back. "What land are we talking about?"

"Half an acre at the east end of town. To the rear of the livery stable."

"What on earth would I do with that?"

Curtis shrugged. "That would be up to you. But if Trinidad expands, as it seems likely to, with the railroad's interest in this town? That property could become quite valuable."

York was shaking his head, as if trying to clear it of cob-webs. "That makes no sense! George Cullen was foursquare against the Santa Fe in this."

The lawyer shrugged, tossing the document on the

table. "This bequest was arranged well before the issue of the railroad spur arose. He felt Trinidad was bound to expand as long as the Bar-O continued to flourish. After all, George Cullen was responsible for this town's very existence."

York's head bobbed back, like he was ducking a blow. "How do you figure that, Counselor?"

Curtis leaned forward, gesturing with an open palm. "The land on which this very town was built was once part of the Bar-O's holdings. Ask Mr. Parker here. He can confirm as much."

Bewildered, York glanced at the businessman, who nodded.

Parker said calmly, "The Bar-O land was purchased many years ago from the holder of a Spanish land grant, for virtual pennies. That included the flat stretch on which Trinidad now stands. I was in charge of the effort to build structures here and invite merchants in, selling to them at a loss. We wanted a town nearby. Going twenty-five or thirty miles for supplies was just too much trouble."

York let out a humorless laugh from deep in his belly. "No wonder the old man was bitter," he said, "when the Citizens Committee wouldn't respect his wishes where the Santa Fe was concerned. He'd practically made a gift of the town to them."

Parker nodded. "But George was wrongheaded in this, nonetheless. Trinidad will wind up just another ghost town if Ellis or Roswell gets the Santa Fe spur."

York could not argue with that.

Half an hour was spent on paperwork, including the transfer of the deed to the east-of-town property. Hands were again shaken all around, and soon York and Parker were back out on the boardwalk.

Parker paused to light up a cigarette. "Any notions for what you might do with your newfound holdings?"

"None. As far as I'm concerned, it's an annoyance. The old boy might have asked me if I was interested in being a damn land owner."

Waving out his match, Parker said, "Most people wouldn't object to such a burden. But I may have a notion for you. I'll be in town till tomorrow. We'll talk again."

And Parker headed across the street, skirting a buckboard, leaving York behind.

The sheriff, hands on his hips, was feeling flummoxed. But then something that had been said at the café made its way from the back of his brain to the front, and he hustled across the street himself.

York pushed through the door into the telegraph office, where skinny, bespectacled Ralph Parsons was behind the counter.

"Sheriff," the operator said.

"Mr. Parsons," the sheriff said.

He filled out a blank form, taking his time, then handed it to the operator.

"Get that right out," York said.

"Will do, Sheriff. Quite a few words."

"I'll pay you for them."

"The Kansas State Penitentiary! My. This sounds serious."

"It is, Ralph. Would you like to know how serious?"

"If you think it's best, Sheriff."

York leaned across the counter and summoned his nastiest smile. "Should you reveal the contents to anyone, I might have to beat you to within an inch of your life."

"But . . . you're the *sheriff*!"

"That's right. And that puts you in a difficult spot, Ralph. Because that leaves only Deputy Tulley to arrest me, and I'd fire him first."

That apparently sank in quickly, because the operator's fingers were flying even before York had stepped outside.

CHAPTER THIRTEEN

Friday, just before eight o'clock, the Victory was jumping, which was not unusual, and yet the place didn't seem itself.

As Caleb York pushed through the batwing doors into the imposing saloon with its fancy high tin ceiling and kerosene chandeliers, he found merchants, clerks, menial workers, and cowboys shoulder to shoulder at the long well-polished carved oaken bar at left, attended by a double-size staff of bow-tied, white-shirt-wearing bartenders. At the rear the small dance floor was packed with dance-hall girls and their customers jigging to a lively tune from the barrelhouse piano player. In the central casino area, stations for dice, faro, red dog, and twenty-one were doing business as usual, but roulette, chuck-a-luck, and wheel of fortune were shut down.

At York's immediate right, tables and chairs normally arranged for the pleasure of drinking men were positioned in clusters to face three round green-felt-topped tables, set well enough apart that the seated spectators might have been viewing three separate theatrical stages lined along the far wall, each with plenty of breathing room.

Those spectator tables and chairs were filled not only with menfolk of Trinidad, but in many cases by their distaff counterparts, as well, gentle creatures not often seen . . . almost *never* seen . . . on these premises, which were, after all, an exclusive male preserve.

Exclusive, of course, but for owner Rita Filley and her dance-hall girls, whose satin and lace and low bodices were in direct contrast to the calico and gingham and high collars of these rare Victory visitors, women whose lack of Sunday-best apparel said something of their attitudes, although the daily wear they sported was clean and crisp and, one might say, wholesome.

As he wandered in, York couldn't help but grin, pushing his hat back on his head, though the smile didn't last long, as he spotted Alver Hollis and his two cronies huddled over by the staircase to Rita's quarters, near one of the trio of green-felt tables. Spotted around the crowd, as well, were various of the city fathers whom York had not long ago interrogated concerning a murder.

Rita herself, in dark blue satin and black lace but sporting less daring a bodice than usual, was threading through the crowd, speaking to the cowboy and town regulars and then winding through the spectator tables to welcome the women gracing her establishment, and their husbands, too, of course. From the ladies, Rita harvested an array of stiff, polite nods before she spotted York standing near, though not at, the bar.

She came over fluidly and stood with her arms folded across the generous shelf of mostly clad bosom and smiled. "Ready for the big game?"

York nodded. "A private word?"

"Of course."

He held one of the batwing doors open for her, and she slipped out. He followed. The night was as crisp as the calico and gingham dresses of the Trinidad wives in attendance, and almost as cold.

"I want to thank you," he said as they stood to one side of the entry, "for providing me with that list of names."

As promised, she had sent over a complete listing of the eighteen players in the draw-poker tournament. With six seats available at each table, that had been the limit.

"Ten locals," York said, "including myself and damn near all the town fathers—mayor, druggist, hardware and mercantile store owners, newspaper editor, even the undertaker."

Shrugging, she asked, "Does that surprise you? Who else in Trinidad could afford the hundred-dollar buy in? And each one has promised, if the winner, to donate the two thousand dollars at stake for the building of a schoolhouse. That's why you have so many wives gracing my tawdry establishment on this fine night."

"Makes sense. And I see Raymond Parker is on the list, as well."

She nodded. "Not a local, but local ties. He's made the same schoolhouse pledge."

"Which, I would imagine, can't be said of the Preacherman and his two choirboys."

A wry smile appeared on the lush red-rouged lips. "No. And the same is true of the remaining seven. We have several professional gamblers, a couple of small ranchers from around Las Vegas, a saloon owner from Ellis, and, well, you get the idea."

"But do you?"

She frowned in confusion. "You're going to have to spell it out, Sheriff. I'm not following you."

He nodded toward the saloon. "You know how the Preacherman operates. He's a hired gun, but he always gets away with it because he stages his kills as fair fights . . . fair fights grown out of disagreements, such as if somebody's been cheating at cards. I know of three men he gunned down in just that manner."

Still frowning, she shook her head. "The mayor and the others . . . they won't be armed. You ever remember seeing any of them with a gun on his hip?"

"No. But that won't matter."

The dark eyes flashed. "But of course it will!"

"No. I'll be armed, and so will the Preacherman and his little gang, and some of the other players. *Not* the city fathers."

Incredulity colored a smile. "If one of them is his intended victim, what would Alver Hollis do? Gun them down in cold blood?"

"That's exactly what he'll do. In at least two previous instances, Hollis was first to his fallen adversary, to bend over and check for vitals . . . and to point out a derringer in the freshly dead man's vest or coat pocket."

"Which he claimed the man had reached for."

He nodded once.

The big brown eyes tightened. "Meaning it was anything *but* a fair fight. That his opponent . . . his victim . . . was unarmed."

"And Hollis planted the little gun on each of them, yes." York's shrug was slow. "Now, it's not always been that way. Preacherman's very fast, they say, and real good at goading a man into going for his gun."

The blood had drained from her face. "You think he's going to kill somebody tonight—here at the Victory."

Another nod. "I think he plans to. That's why I had

you seat me at his table. I want to be right on top of things."

"Understood." She sighed deeply, shuddering and not entirely because of the chill. "Now I'm regretting not using Cole and a couple of his professional pals."

House dealer Yancy Cole would not be dealing and would instead be a kind of roving referee—this would be strictly a player-dealt game, the entrants at each table passing the deck after their deal. That decision had unwittingly paved the way for one player to accuse another of cheating while dealing.

Also, when the players at a table were reduced to two, as the others lost and departed, those top two players would move into seats made available by losers at the other two tables. Eventually, there would be one table, and one winner. And the process might last a very long time, probably longer than the visiting ladies could endure, even at the prospect of a schoolhouse.

"You're right in thinking," York told her, "that one of the players here tonight is the Preacherman's target."

The pretty eyes were hidden in slits now. "And not any of the out-of-towners."

"Probably not. Likely one of our city fathers. Possibly Raymond Parker, particularly if the George Cullen murder was the work of the Preacherman, too."

"I don't follow."

He grunted something deep in his belly that wasn't exactly a laugh. "Cullen's murder guaranteed his partner and oldest friend, Raymond Parker, would come to town for the services. But I'm not sure how anyone could make the leap that Parker would stay for the poker tourney, as well. Perhaps our friend from Denver was somehow manipulated into participating."

She shook her head. "I have no way of knowing. He simply came into the Victory the evening of the Cullen burial and asked to be added to the list. I had a seat left, and I gave it to him."

York looked toward the saloon, from which raucous music could barely be heard under the conversation and laughter.

"Well," he said, "Hollis is here to kill *somebody*. So I'll do my best to stay in the game and follow him to the table where his potential victim is seated."

"You play well, Caleb, but there's no guarantee of that."

"No, there isn't," he admitted.

She shivered, hugged her arms to herself. "This is terrible. Some innocent bystander could be shot!"

He rested a gentle hand on her bare shoulder; it was warm, even if she wasn't.

"Probably not," he said reassuringly, squeezing her shoulder, then removing his hand. "The Preacherman's a professional. But that's a valid concern. And he's backed up by those other two reprobates, so it is possible bullets could fly."

"Oh, my God." It was almost a prayer.

Nodding toward the Victory, he said, "There are still a few audience tables open in there, despite the crowd. Grab one for me, would you, before somebody at the bar comes over and fills it? And move it into the front row?"

"Of course. Why?"

"I'm going to position Tulley with a shotgun on his lap in full view of the players. Encouraging caution on their part. And I'll have Doc Miller seated, with his medical bag under the table. We'll be ready for anything. . . . Here they come now."

Footsteps on the boardwalk announced the bandy-legged deputy and Doc Miller, his suit looking pressed for once, chugging toward them. Tulley's scattergun was cradled, and the doctor's bag was in hand.

A hand on York's sleeve, Rita asked, "Anything else I can do?"

"Tell Yancy Cole what's going on. He isn't wearing a sidearm. Have him sling one on. Were you planning on table service?"

"Yes. I was going to use one of my girls. . . ." She grinned impishly. "Just to sort of rattle the holier-than-thou ladies."

"Use Hub Wainwright instead. And tell him to have a gun stuck in his belt under his apron."

"My lord, you make it sound like a war is coming."

"No. A battle, maybe."

She shuddered, nodded, and quickly pushed her way back inside.

York waited for Tulley and Doc Miller, to give them instructions. So far all he'd told them was just to meet him here.

After he'd given them their directions, Doc Miller said, "Seems like everywhere you go, Caleb, a physician ought to follow."

"And yet," York said, "I get no share in the fee."

Soon the stage was set, with York himself part of it. He was seated across from Alver Hollis, with pop-eyed Lafe Trammel to the man's right, one cheek covered by a bandage now, and porky Wilbur Landrum to the left. The Preacherman was in his usual black, his hat on, and his partners were in battered hats, arm-gartered work shirts, and bandanas no less filthy for the occasion. Each had his small stacks of one hundred dollars' worth of chips before him—white bone chips edged blue (ten dollars), red (five dollars), orange (two dollars), and natural white (one dollar).

Also seated with York and the Preacherman flock were undertaker Perkins and *Enterprise* editor Penniman, everyone with their little towers of chips, whites tallest, blues shortest. Two Bicycle decks were in front of York, who had drawn first deal when house dealer Cole—in his trademark white, round-brimmed hat, gray suit, and ruffled shirt—came around and had each player draw for high card.

York exchanged smiles with all the men, even Hollis, although his idiot companions just scowled.

The next table over included Mayor Hardy, Newt Harris, and Raymond Parker, and three out-of-towners, two who were likely ranchers and another whose riverboat gambler apparel marked him as a professional. The table beyond that one included Clarence Mathers, Clem Davis, several area small ranchers, and more nonlocals.

The tables were spaced far enough apart that players at one table would have to damn near yell to be heard by the next. A good six feet had been allowed between the green-topped ones and tables occupied by the seated audience, who must have approached one hundred.

But down at the street end, almost to the front windows, one table had been slid between the front row of spectators and the wall. There sat Jonathan R. Tulley, who had finally bought a shirt—gray flannel—to wear over his BVD top, his scattergun nestled in his lap like a loyal dog. Next to the deputy sat Dr. Albert Miller, his Gladstone bag at his feet.

Well, Caleb York thought, *with the deputy, doctor,*

undertaker, and newspaper editor all close at hand, every contingency should be covered.

Cole, friendly and handsome in his skinny-mustached way, strode to the front of the seated audience and raised his palms to quiet them.

"Ladies and gentlemen," the house dealer said in a Southern drawl that might have been genuine, though York wouldn't have bet more than a white chip on it, "welcome to the Victory. Ladies, we are particularly pleased to have you brighten up our lowly establishment, and perhaps in future we can find entertainment more suitable to your gentle sensibilities."

The wives of Trinidad mostly smiled at that, and a few even blushed.

"I will be supervising tonight's games," Cole said, "to assure one and all that this is an honest, well-intended endeavor on the part of the Victory and these players. And now I'd like to introduce you to your hostess, Miss Rita Filley."

Gesturing openhandedly, Cole made way for Rita, who took center stage to applause that was merely polite, since the husbands dared not clap too loudly and the women barely clapped at all.

"Welcome," she said in a strong, clear voice. "We have separated our three tables in order to provide you good people a better opportunity to follow the action. Our players have been instructed to call out their bets and their requests for additional cards, as well as their hands when laying them down at the conclusion of betting."

With considerable grace, Rita moved up and down the edge of the audience. Eyes male and female followed her.

"If you have difficulty hearing any of our competitors," she continued, "please page Mr. Cole, the gentleman who just spoke to you, who will be monitoring the action. He will do his best to rectify the situation. We do ask you to watch quietly, as draw poker is a game requiring considerable concentration, and we are already subjecting our players to a circumstance that is unusual, to say the least."

Now Rita again deposited herself at center stage.

"I must add," she said, "that we have no way of knowing how long our tournament may last, and we understand that you may need to leave temporarily or for the evening, should we extend into the wee hours. As Mr. Cole mentioned, we are pleased to see with us this evening so many of our lovely Trinidad ladies, who are likely, as am I, to be rooting for a new schoolhouse . . . thanks to the participation of our Citizens Committee and our guest Raymond L. Parker of Denver."

Those players, at Rita's urging, stood and half bowed, and a solid round of applause echoed off the tin ceiling.

Then Rita said with her own half bow, "Thank you, gentlemen . . . and ladies."

This time the applause for their hostess was perhaps more than polite, though still not ringing.

Cole called out, "Gentlemen . . . you may begin play!"

As York shuffled, he considered how key it would be for the Preacherman to win and keep winning, should his intended target be at one of the adjoining tables. As he dealt, he wondered who among these city fathers might be that target.

In the West, one never knew the history of a seemingly upstanding citizen. Only the background of editor Penniman, who had worked in the newspaper trade for some time, was known to York. But he could certainly have made a powerful enemy in that pursuit.

And who could say what sin lurked in the past of the undertaker here, a man so comfortable with death? Or whom the druggist, Davis, might have accidentally or even purposely poisoned? Had the barber or the hardware man stolen money or swindled a partner elsewhere to set up shop in New Mexico? That mercantile store would take real money to get going.

Who is the target?

The first hand was won by Hollis—three jacks taking it over York's pair of aces, the others having dropped out. With an ante of a dollar chip, a first round two-dollar bet, and York meeting the Preacherman's five-dollar bet, that was twenty-eight dollars sliding down to Hollis at his end of the table, with York eight dollars the poorer.

This could go fast, he thought.

But things evened out as each player took his turn as dealer. York noted that when Hollis first dealt—and the Preacherman had a riverboat gambler's touch that Yancy Cole might have envied—lanky, bandaged Trammel pulled in a pot with the best hand of the night so far: full house, queens over tens.

Both Trammel and Landrum had to be reminded when they displayed their hands to announce their cards to the crowd, but by the time the cards came around to York again, they'd fallen in line. York's deal this time earned him a small victory—a pair of kings besting the undertaker's eights—and by the start of the second hour, he was up fifteen dollars. Trammel was keeping alive, largely based on that big pot he'd landed, though Landrum's stacks had dwindled considerably.

Down half maybe?

Then it was the Preacherman's deal and, lo and behold, Landrum pulled in his own healthy pot, with a straight to

the king, which knocked out York's three queens and decent hands that had kept both Perkins and Penniman in
for several raises. Their stacks were withering. Only
Trammel had been smart enough to get out.

Trammel smart enough?

That was the moment when York realized how Hollis
was operating. Whenever the deal was his, the Preacherman was feeding big pots to Trammel and Landrum to
keep them in the game. Hollis was sharp enough a player
not to have to cheat for his own benefit, at least not at
this point.

But the way the tournament was set up, only two players from this table would move on to the next one. *So
why keep them both in?* Why didn't the Preacherman se-
lect one of his cronies—the better gun between them,
most likely—to move on to the next table with him?

Something at the back of York's neck was tingling.

The deck was his now. He shuffled four times, gave the
cards to Penniman for a cut, then began to deal. When he
looked at his cards, they almost smiled back at him—an
ace-high flush. A lovely hand. Hollis opened for two dollars. Everybody stayed in, and York raised it another orange chip.

Again, everybody stayed.

Nobody liked it when York said he was pat, but nonetheless, everybody stayed in for the second round of betting.
That could make uneasy even a player with a hand as good
as York's. He decided to see where the power was and
raised Penniman, who had bet two more dollars, a red-
edged chip. Five whole dollars.

At that, everybody dropped out but the Preacherman,
who saw the five and raised it ten—the first raise of a
blue-edged chip at this table. York saw the bet and raised

it another blue chip—the final bet allowed. All eyes at the table traveled between the two men, and the audience near their table was paying rapt attention, as well.

Hollis saw York's ten dollars and raised it another blue chip.

And York knew. Suddenly he knew. Knew exactly who the Preacherman had come to town to kill . . .

Caleb York.

Casually, he dropped his right hand from the table as he flipped with his left another blue chip into the pot, seeing Hollis's bet.

"Three kings," Hollis said, showing them.

York turned over the ace-high flush.

And just as he knew would happen, the Preacherman snarled, "You're a goddamned *cheater*, York! You been dealing off the bottom, and my friends and me *saw* it!"

The Preacherman's right hand slipped from view.

With his left, York upended the table, putting it between him and Hollis, and chips and cards flew everywhere, and the players to his right and left scattered almost as quickly as the .44 in Caleb York's fist punched three holes through the table in the Preacherman's general direction.

The thunder of it, the splintering wood, the smoke from the gun, the shrieks of women, the yells from men were everywhere as York, ready to shoot again, kicked his chair away and stepped to his left.

Hollis crawled out from behind and under the upended table, Colt .45 in hand, and rolled onto his side, tried to bring the gun up, hand quavering, then passed out.

The Preacherman's stunned gunny Trammel backed away, eyes bulging, and bumped into the staircase, going for his own .45 as an afterthought. York sent a shot through the goggle-eyed scarecrow's right shoulder, rocking him, turning his gun hand a limp thing that could barely hold on to its fingers let alone a weapon, which careened away on the floor somewhere. Then Trammel lost his balance and sat down hard on a stair step and slid down to the next one and sat hard again.

Somewhere an explosion happened, and York glanced to his right to see that the pig-faced Landrum, .45 in hand, had taken a blast from Tulley's scattergun in the back and was weaving on two pudgy legs that did not have a chance in hell of holding him up. In the next instant the pudgy saddle tramp flopped facedown onto the back of the table, cracking it, the bloody, jagged, gaping hole in his back revealing his spine had indeed been severed.

York had barely heard the screams of the men and women who had been so nearby and were now down on the floor, knocking chairs aside, scrambling away like the frightened animals they'd become. And he did not see Rita Filley watching with big eyes and a hand over her mouth. Nor did he see Hub Wainwright and Yancy Cole coming up with their weapons in hand, ready to back him, if he needed it.

He didn't.

York went over to the Preacherman, who was on his back now, hat askew, his breathing heavy and bubbling, mouth frothing scarlet, two red holes in his black-vested chest and another in his belly, and plucked the .45 from the dying man's fingers.

Turned out the ivory handles did have angels carved on them.

York stuffed the gun in his waistband just as Hollis's eyes fluttered open. Then the killer's face contorted into something ugly with pain and hate, though it included a terrible grin. A slight bob of the head bid York to lean closer, which he did.

"See you . . . see you in hell," the Preacherman whispered.

"I don't remember that one," York said. "What's that? Proverbs? Psalms?"

Then the Preacherman's grin was gone, and so was he.

To his final reward.

CHAPTER FOURTEEN

At just after eight o'clock the next morning, Caleb York entered his jailhouse office to the unmistakable aroma of his deputy's coffee. Always strong enough to curl the bark off a tree, the stuff had taken some getting used to, but York had come to depend on it to get his day going, after coming straight over from the hotel without taking breakfast yet to check with Tulley and see if anything had come up overnight.

After the shooting at the Victory last night, he expected news this morning.

He got it.

Tulley, a York-designated tin cup of Arbuckles' in hand, rushed over from his table to set the coffee down and lean in like a friendly madman. The nice shirt of the night before was gone, and the skinny, bowlegged deputy was back to a badge-pinned BVD top and suspenders.

"That feller you shot last night? One ye didn't kill?"

"I vaguely recall," York said after braving a sip.

The white-bearded coot thrust out a finger, pointing toward the lockup. "He's back in the cell next to mine."

Tulley was not a prisoner—exactly—but did regularly

camp out on the cot in a cell, keeping the office manned through the night.

York sipped again. Few things made him wince in pain, but this bitter brew did just that.

"Trammel," he said.

"Yep. Lafe Trammel. The doc brought him over round midnight, all bandaged up and loopy on laudanum. Trammel, I mean, not the doc. I deposited him in that cell. Slept good. Didn't bother me none."

If Tulley's own lumber-mill-in-action snoring hadn't woken their guest, then Doc Miller must have administered a pretty good slug of the morphine/alcohol mix that was laudanum.

Tulley pressed a hand on the desk and leaned forward, keeping his voice hushed. "But our guest woke up this mornin', when the Mexie's roosters 'cross the way started in to crowin'. He was blubberin', Sheriff—blubberin' like a baby."

"Do tell."

Tulley jerked a thumb toward the cells. "He's scared, Sheriff. From them spooky eyes down to his dirty toes. Now, when I checked on him bit ago and give him a walk out to the privy, he got cocky again. All tough talk. 'Bout how he'd make you pay for gunnin' down his Preacherman pal."

Another bracing sip. "So what do you make of it, Tulley?"

"Jest braggadocio. The no-good's scared of what's goin' to happen to him. Scared of what *you* might do to him."

"Good to know, Tulley. Good to know."

Tulley nodded, grinning, self-satisfied, then headed back to his table and his own tin cup of eye-opener. When he'd settled in his chair, something came to him, and he called out, "Oh! That envelope there—Ralph Parsons from the telegraph office dropped that by first thing!"

York, who hadn't noticed it atop a pile of circulars, plucked off the little yellow envelope and had a look inside. As he read, he smiled slowly to himself, then folded and tucked the telegram into his breast pocket. He finished his coffee, then headed back to the cell where Lafe Trammel sat slumped on the edge of his cot, which was chained to the wall.

The lanky gunhand had his right arm in a sling, and his hat was beside him on the blanket, but otherwise he looked the same—bulging eyed and scruffy, though his filthy shirt and bandana and trousers bore some reddish-brown bloodstains. The doc had given him a fresh bandage, a little smaller, for his cheek.

"What the hell charge you holdin' me for, York?" the prisoner blustered, getting to his feet and coming over to the bars. "After you shot my partner, I was jest meanin' to protect myself."

York found a chair and dragged it over. Sat. "You know, Lafe, you have a point. It's within my power to take you at your word and send you on your way. If I did, you'd have no reason to hang around Trinidad, would you now?"

Had those eyes grown any wider, they'd have fallen out of Trammel's head and gone rolling around on the floor.

"You got *nothin'* in this town I give a good goddamn about! You spring Mrs. Trammel's baby boy, and the ass end of my horse is the last you'll see of me!"

York nodded slowly, as if considering the offer. "On the other hand, you've been traveling in the company of Alver Hollis and that fellow Landrum, may they both rest in peace or not . . . and of course, Hollis was a known hired gun."

"Never proved. Never proved."

"If I were to tell the circuit judge that you drew down on me in a gunfight you and the Preacherman and Landrum started, before witnesses . . . well, the only question is whether you'd get a rope or a prison cell."

The pop eyes popped. "A rope! I didn't kill nobody!"

York made a fatalistic click in one cheek. "You drew down on a lawman. We hang you for that in this territory." York didn't know if that was true, but he made it sound so.

Trammel hung onto the bars of his cell as if they were all that was holding him up. "Turn me loose, Sheriff. Turn me loose, and you won't see hide nor hair of me again."

York was shaking his head glumly. "I can't have the good folks of Trinidad thinking a man can pull on me and I just let him get away with it."

Trammel shook the bars, and they rattled some. "*I'm* the one got shot! I didn't get away with *nothin'*!"

"You *are* the one who got shot," York granted, pointing a forefinger at the prisoner. "You might have been killed."

"I might have been!"

"But you weren't. I didn't kill you, like I did the Preacherman. Like my deputy did Landrum. What do you make of that, Lafe?"

The goggly eyes drifted. "You . . . you missed?"

York grinned at him. "Really? You know my reputation. Do you really think Caleb York would miss at such close range?"

A thought worked to form, then, "You winged me on . . . on purpose?"

"I did."

Trammel shook his head. "What for, Sheriff? *I'da* killed me in your place. It ain't like you ain't a killer yourself. The Preacherman said you was one right dangerous son of a . . . buck."

York shrugged. "Maybe I wanted you alive."

Trammel made a face. "Why would you want a no-good drifter like me to keep breathin'?"

"Possibly to answer a question or two."

The prisoner's big eyes went half lidded, like a stage curtain that couldn't come all the way down.

York went on. "Possibly, I might trade you your freedom for some answers."

The curtains on the eyes came down farther, leaving only a pair of skeptical slits. "I'm listenin'."

"Good. Because I'm asking. Who was your target in town?"

Trammel's lips flapped with escaping air. "You know the answer to that one already, Sheriff. *You* was! But not no more. With the Preacherman gone, I sure as hell ain't gonna go up against you."

"Not even bushwhacking me from around a building or crouched down in back of a barrel?"

"No, sir! You let me go, I'm gone. Nothing left but my dust."

York nodded thoughtfully. "Okay, then. Last question. Who hired the Preacherman? Who wants me dead?"

The prisoner swallowed. "That kinda sounds like two questions."

"No. It's just one."

Trammel shook his head and gave up a rumpled, somewhat toothless grin. "Sheriff, that ain't the way things worked with the Preacherman. He never told us where the money come from. He was kinda like . . . protectin' the client. . . . That's what he called them types, the client. . . . And, hell, he didn't tell us jack about who the target was till a day or two afore."

"Why?"

Trammel shrugged. "I dunno. Said somethin' a time or two about . . . well, about idiots always runnin' at the mouth."

"Meaning you and Landrum."

"Meanin' us two. He was always funnin' like that."

"Yeah," York said. "I noticed his sense of humor. And I believe you when you say he wanted to protect his clients. That you would not be privy to that piece of information. In most cases."

The slits returned. "What do you mean, Sheriff . . . 'in most cases'?"

York dug out the telegram from his breast pocket. "Can you read, Lafe?"

His stubbly chin came up defensively. "I had near two year of schoolin'. Enough to make out what I need to."

York held up the telegram, and Trammel pushed his face between the bars and read, moving his lips. Slowly.

Then the prisoner said, "The Kansas State Pen, huh? Warden hisself."

York gave the man a slow, easy grin. "You want another crack at my question, Lafe? Since I think we both know the answer."

Trammel sighed, nodded, and talked.

In his usual Earp brothers black, York tied up the gray gelding at the hitching post in front of the Bar-O ranch house. Mid-morning now, things were quiet, all the hands out in the continuing preparation for even colder weather than today's, which was plenty nippy and un-usually overcast for New Mexico.

He went up the short flight of stairs to the porch, spurs ajangle. Toward the far end, down from the fancy carved front door, he began examining the rough bark-and-all overhang posts. What he had in mind was a piece of overdue detective work, based upon his reflections on the nature of George Cullen's head wound.

And there it was.

On the second post from the end, at a height perhaps a head shorter than Cullen, perfect for if the man had been shoved back and knocked hard into it, leaving a smear of what had now long since dried and gone crusty maroon . . .

Blood.

Almost certainly human. Short of a bird flying straight into it, how might this post have come in contact with any other kind?

The front door opened, and York turned to see Burt O'Malley step out and regard him quizzically. The fifty-ish Bar-O cofounder wore the same apparel he'd shown up in—blue shirt, brown vest, red bandana. Hatless, though. He again wore Levi's, and his hip bore no hol-stered weapon. The oblong face with its dark blue eyes, trim salt-and-pepper beard, and easygoing smile seemed friendly as ever.

"Caleb? If you're here to see Willa, she went out for a ride. She's been doing that purt' near every morning since her pa died."

"Come take a look at this, Burt."

The big man loped down and had a gander where York was pointing.

York asked, "What's that look like to you?"

"Can't say. Some kind of dirt. Food spill from the other day, when half the world was out here, could be."

"Blood maybe?"

O'Malley shrugged. "Maybe."

The two men were only a couple of feet apart.

York said, "I told you that you were seen arguing with the old man out here. That it got physical. Maybe you grabbed him and knocked his head against that post— hard enough to really make your point. An accident, possibly . . . or possibly not an accident."

O'Malley smiled in strained patience. "Don't talk nonsense. Anyhow, that argument was the night before and wasn't even really an argument a'tall. Nothin' that came to blows."

"So you said."

"I was just trying to make the old boy see that maybe he should give a little more thought to taking advantage of that spur goin' in, since if he didn't cooperate, it would go in without him all the same."

York raised an eyebrow. "If he didn't go along with it, that branchline would still go in, all right . . . but the cost to the Santa Fe would be much higher, having to skirt this spread and hopscotch through the small independent ranchers."

O'Malley shrugged. "Exactly right. That's why George could've got even more money out of the railroad than they was offerin'. Come on now, Caleb . . . Sheriff . . . you can't be serious that I'd ever harm that man. I owed him plenty. And besides that, I loved that stubborn old soul."

"You may have loved him once upon a time . . . only maybe all those years behind bars changed you. It can do that to a man. And at your age, an opportunity to, well, make a killing? That don't come along every day."

The friendliness was out of O'Malley's face now, but only a weariness had taken its place—not the rage York had expected.

"Let's get in out of the cold," the big man said with a sigh that was visible in the late-autumn air. "There's a fire going. Let's sit and talk this out like civilized men."

York didn't have a hell of a lot to go on where the Cullen murder was concerned. That dried maroon smear. The potential testimony of the foreman, Whit Murphy, who really hadn't seen much. But on another matter, he had plenty.

"All right," York said. "Let's go inside."

The fire was going, providing a nice warmth to the long, narrow room, which would have seemed cozy under other circumstances. Each man took one of the rough-wood chairs that long ago George Cullen had fashioned.

O'Malley said, "There's coffee on the stove."

"No thanks."

"Maybe somethin' stronger?"

"Too early."

"Mind if I get something for myself, Sheriff?"

"I do. Just stay put. I don't mind getting in out of the cold, but I have no intention of letting you go off and arm yourself."

"You're still suspicious."

"More than just suspicious."

York removed the folded telegram from his breast pocket and handed it over, then watched as O'Malley opened it up and read. His face fell as he did; then a smile formed, but not that easygoing one that all who'd encountered him of late had come to know.

York said, his voice quiet and businesslike, "The warden at the Kansas State Pen at Lansing confirms that you shared a cell with Lafe Trammel for two years. He was released a few months before you."

"This doesn't prove a damn thing."

"Not about George Cullen's murder. But it suggests that you were the one who hired Alver Hollis to come to Trinidad and blow a hole or two through this hide of mine."

The smile settled on one side of O'Malley's face. "And why would I do that?"

"I admit that took me a while. That's the kind of thing that can keep a man up at night, thinkin'. I mean, what threat did I pose to you?"

"Exactly."

"Then it came to me. You were sent here by agents of the Santa Fe Railroad. They had done their research and learned that one of the original three owners of the Bar-O was serving a sentence for manslaughter. They looked you up and got you out and signed you on. Your job was to come to the Bar-O and get back in the old man's good graces. That fight you had with that big lug Lem, sticking up for Cullen, that was a nice touch."

The half smile lingered. "Let's say that's so, Sheriff . . . for the sake of argument. How does that make you somebody I'd want dead?"

"Like I said, the Santa Fe folks had done their research. Their man Prescott in particular was thick with the local Citizens Committee. Prescott learned that I was close to both George and Willa Cullen."

"Meaning what?"

"Meaning the assumption was that I would back up

whatever position George Cullen took—which, of course, was against the spur. The other assumption was that I might bring Willa Cullen around to her father's way of thinking, when certain locals knew she was otherwise leaning in favor of the spur. And what if Willa and I were to wed? *I'd* be the new man on the Bar-O, and where would that leave you and your plans? Removing me from the equation—and this, I believe, was your idea, because Prescott and the Santa Fe would likely stop short of murder—would put you, Uncle Burt, the prodigal returned, in an ideal position to agree with Willa and bring her father around."

"What, and if he didn't, then I'd murder him? Absurd."

"It's true I can't, right now, anyway, think of how I'd prove that. Hell of it is, I was pretty much in favor of that branchline coming in myself. So all your efforts to have me removed were pointless. Anyway, I have an ace in the hole. An ugly, scruffy ace, but an ace, nonetheless."

"And what would that be?"

"Not what, Burt. *Who*. Damnedest thing . . . You know who can read some? You'd never guess it. Lafe Trammel! He read that same telegram you did, and admitted that he was the one who put you and the Preacherman together. That you were the client, and I was the target."

O'Malley's grin was gone.

York went on. "So I guess, for now, I'll just have to settle for attempted murder on your part. Much as I'd like to put your neck in a noose, I'll have to settle for another nice long prison sentence. You know, New Mexico's building its own prison now, and maybe you'll be in line for a spanking new cell. Kind of fittingly, it's in Santa Fe."

The two men just sat there for a while, reflections of orange and blue flames lazily licking at their faces. Finally, O'Malley swung his face toward York, and his smile was back, and this time it was damn near satanic.

"See where you get with this fairy tale, York. You have a saddle tramp who's dumber than a cactus, and I'll have the Santa Fe Railroad and all its money and influence behind me."

York shook his head. "I don't think so. I don't think they'll claim you, not after the things you pulled in their name. When I met with Prescott, he was already backing away from you."

"Is this true?"

The voice came from just behind York. *Willa!* She must have come in the back way, maybe after dropping off Daisy at the barn rather than hitching her out front.

O'Malley's face, with the flame reflections dripping down, might have been made of melting wax. But his expression betrayed no anger or fear, rather . . . York tried to read it. *Disappointment?*

And a sudden realization came to York: what O'Malley had wanted all along was to regain his life here at the Bar-O, his place in this world. He probably *had* felt affection for George Cullen, and for Willa, too, a father-daughter feeling denied a man who had spent too much of his life in a prison cell.

Half out of his chair, O'Malley asked softly, "How much did you hear, child?"

"I heard everything from the moment the two of you sat down!"

"Surely, you don't believe—"

She stalked over to him, her fists balled, her body quivering with rage. "I believe every word of it. Caleb York has the instincts not just of a friend of this family, but of a detective, and he—"

But then O'Malley was on his feet, and he grabbed her around the waist and swung the girl in front of him, facing York, a human shield.

York was on his feet, too, and his hand was inches away from the holstered .44 when O'Malley reached behind him and took down the old Sharps buffalo gun from its deer-hoof rack, then aimed it alongside Willa, its barrel a long accusatory finger pointed right at York.

"This is no decorative item," O'Malley reminded him, grinning like a prisoner getting the best of a guard. "I know the old man kept it loaded."

"There's not enough of her for you to hide behind," York said. "You put that gun down now, or I'll put a bullet in you before you can use it. Just toss it on that chair!"

"No. You need a head shot, and I ain't givin' you one."

And indeed O'Malley was ducked down enough for Willa to cover all but a sliver of his face.

"Here's how this is going to go," O'Malley said, his voice matter of fact and as cold as that day out there. "I'm walking your precious Willa to the door, and then she and I will go out together. When I get to my horse, I'll let her go. I'm fond of her. I won't kill her if I don't have to."

"You think you can get that far?"

Willa was breathing hard, her eyes and nostrils flaring.

"I do," said the man with the rifle. "Because you're going to unbuckle that gun belt and let it fall. Do it. *Now!*"

Grimacing, York undid the belt and let it drop to the floor with a nasty, clanking thud.

"Step out of it," O'Malley instructed.

York did.

"Kick it away. Well away!"

York did that, too.

O'Malley started backing toward the door, with Willa still between him and the unarmed York, her captor's arm up from around her waist and now across her breasts to grip a shoulder and better drag her.

"Now, just stay put, Sheriff York. You'll have her back soon enough."

York figured his best play was to let them get out the door, then to grab his gun and throw himself through the front window onto the porch. He was calculating how to get to his gun quickly and back again when Willa bit down hard on the hand of the arm at her shoulder and at the same time brought her right boot heel down on O'Malley's right foot, like a child in a tantrum.

The big man yowled and let loose of her enough that she squirmed away and threw herself on the floor a good six feet from him. York went for the holstered gun on the floor, got it, came up with the chair he'd been in, which provided some cover, and then the world exploded.

O'Malley stood there with the barrel of the old 50-70 Gov't Sharps peeled back like the skin of a banana, somehow still holding on to the thing, though his right arm and hand were a bloody mess, bone and scorched sinew showing, with flecks of black, sizzling powder spattering the man's face, his mouth open in a silent scream, his eyes wide with pain and surprise. And in his chest were bright orange shards of blowback metal, like the petals of some terrible flower. And when he toppled and hit the floor facedown, those shards of metal were driven even deeper.

Willa was screaming, scrambling to her feet, then backing away, as York approached O'Malley's body, knelt, and looked for a pulse in the man's neck. None was to be found.

York got to his feet and went over and turned Willa away from the grotesque corpse.

Hugging him, she gazed up with wet eyes, her lips trembling. "What . . . what caused it to backfire?"

"I don't know," York admitted. "Must have been twenty years ago or more since your father loaded that weapon. Dirt clog, insect nest, black powder gone bad . . . Who can say? But a lot more backfired for Burt O'Malley today than just that old Sharps."

Yet York could not help but wonder if in some way George Cullen had stepped in to settle things with his old partner.

CHAPTER FIFTEEN

The following Saturday afternoon at the Grange Hall—
a recently built redbrick building that sat on its own
half acre past the church on the road to the cemetery—almost everyone in town and many from the surrounding
area were gathered for a meeting. News had gone out by
way of the *Enterprise* newspaper, posted circulars, and
word of mouth. For those few who had missed it, notices
in every store window in Trinidad, all closed for the
meeting, announced the event: TOWN MEETING – SANTA FE
SPUR.

This afternoon the building's unostentatious interior—
pale green walls, pounded tin ceiling, varnished wood floor,
modest stage—was brimming with citizens and ranch folk,
with children on hand, as well, even babes in arms, whose
occasional squalling was at odds with the generally buoy-
ant mood of the crowd. Many of the townspeople were
dressed as if for church, and even the cowhands were in
relatively clean attire. The unspoken rule here was no
guns, and a table near the door made a temporary home
to a collection of rifles and gun belts.

On the stage, with a podium central, were seated the
members of the Citizens Committee, in dark suits and

bright expressions. Among them were Willa Cullen, in a simple navy-and-white calico dress, her yellow hair piled high, and Santa Fe Railroad representative Grover Prescott, impressive in a gray frock coat and a dark, low-cut vest, with a small big-city bow tie. Next to Prescott was a similarly dressed, similarly eminent-looking Raymond L. Parker.

Caleb York, in his customary black with dudish touches, had been invited, indeed urged, to take a seat onstage but had demurred. It would be enough to sit in the front row and come up and speak his peace. This whole thing was something of an embarrassment to him. Nothing on this earth scared him much, but public speaking challenged that notion.

The mayor introduced Prescott, who took the podium.

"I am pleased to announce," the distinguished figure said, his sonorous voice in tune with his neatly trimmed beard and hawkish countenance, "that an agreement has been reached with Miss Willa Cullen of the Bar-O Ranch for the right-of-way for construction of a Trinidad to Las Vegas branchline."

The hall rang with applause and even some cowhand whoops. Prescott allowed this to go on for some time, not raising a hand to stop the ovation till it threatened to die of its own accord.

This was followed by Prescott repeating, almost word for word, his speech at the Citizens Committee meeting not so long ago, when he told of neighboring Las Vegas having "gone from a bump in the road to a booming community." This went on awhile, though less than before, as on this occasion the sheriff did not interrupt with words of caution about the cons that went with the many pros of the venture.

After all, York was fully on board now. He'd soon have

a pay raise and a house . . . and a lot more on his hands as Trinidad grew, though that prospect didn't bother him much. He didn't mind earning his pay.

And while Prescott and the Santa Fe had by any measure been unscrupulous in their efforts to secure the Bar-O's right of passage, York had seen to it this past week that the railroad paid through the teeth to get the cooperation of one certain young lady.

That young lady Prescott was in the process of introducing right now: Willa approached the podium amid her own round of better than polite applause. She faced the crowd without notes, chin high, her strong, sweet voice easily heard.

"I know that the general opinion in this room is that the Santa Fe spur is a positive thing for our community," she said. "And that has been my feeling from the start, as well. But I know, too, that some of you may wonder how I could take steps in this matter that are contradictory to my late father's wishes."

The hall got very silent.

"My father signed over the Bar-O to me some time ago," she said. "Though I was not the son he would perhaps have preferred, he gave me increasing responsibility over the ranch these past several years. He knew that when the time came that I was on my own, I would operate our business however I thought best . . . and he trusted me in that regard."

Every eye was on her, and even the infants were mute.

She continued. "My father may have lost his sight, but not his vision for this rough-and-tumble part of the world. He wanted what was best not only for the Bar-O but for Trinidad and the entire surrounding region, as well. I believe I would have come to convince him of the merit of the spur, though, of course, I can't be sure. I have to follow my own instincts and desires. But in making this decision, I mean to honor him and the pioneer spirit he represents, and in no way diminish his memory or his name."

She paused, and the room again broke into applause—no whoops this time. This was a respectful response.

"Toward that end," she said, "I wish to turn the podium over to my father's original copartner in the Bar-O, Mr. Raymond L. Parker."

Few here knew much of Parker, but to what degree his name was known, it was viewed in a positive light. Applause greeted him, although the roof was in no risk of being blown off. Willa returned to her chair.

The dignified, white-mustached businessman came to the podium, thanked Willa and Prescott, and the committee, as well, then addressed the crowd.

"Ladies and gentlemen," he said in a voice easily as commanding as Prescott's, "as many of you know, the very land Trinidad rests upon once belonged to the late George Cullen. His goodwill and good intentions brought this town into existence. Many of the fine gentlemen on this stage were given their start when George Cullen encouraged them to be part of this community."

Behind him, the members of the Citizens Committee were nodding.

Parker went on. "As executor of the George O. Cullen estate, I am here to inform you that several adjacent parcels of land to the rear of the town livery stable have been left by Mr. Cullen to your esteemed sheriff, Caleb York."

Murmuring rolled in a wave across the hall. Willa Cullen, who knew nothing of this, sat forward in her chair, frowning in confusion.

"Caleb," Parker said, with a gesture toward the front row, "would you come up and join me?"

York did so, stepping onto the shallow stage, taking a position to one side of the podium.

Parker said, "Sheriff York and I are pleased to announce a joint business venture. That venture involves the Santa Fe Railroad, as well, and some negotiations remain to be concluded . . . but we are confident in the outcome."

Prescott was nodding at this, his smile not betraying the strain of having to deal with Caleb York a second time.

Parker raised his voice a level. "I will be providing the funds for the construction involved, and the sheriff will be providing the land."

The murmuring began again, but Parker silenced it with a raised hand.

"Sheriff," he said, turning to York. "Would you explain to these good people to what end we're pooling our resources?"

York nodded and said to the sea of faces, "Trinidad will soon have a fine new train station. And I'm pleased to say it will be known as the George O. Cullen Depot."

Then, as still more applause rang through the Grange Hall, Willa was suddenly at his side, looking up at him with those lovely blue eyes moist with emotion, taking his hands in hers. Spontaneously, with no thought of where they were, she embraced him. Embarrassed, York looked away and saw something of interest.

Bar-O foreman Whit Murphy rose from a back-row seat and went over to the table of guns, where he selected his holster with gun and cartridge belt, and slipped outside.

Willa released York and, embarrassed herself now, slipped back to her seat, as around her, some good-natured laughter mixed in with the continued clapping. York stepped down from the stage, and Prescott joined Parker at the podium, and they began taking questions from the audience.

Rather than return to his seat, however, York walked down the central aisle, garnering a concerned glance from Rita Filley, seated discreetly toward the back. He gave her a quick nod and went over to pluck his own gun belt from the table of weaponry.

When he stepped outside, he found the weathered, lanky Murphy, the gun on his hip now, about to unhitch his horse from the long post out front of the hall. No one else was around; the hard-dirt road was nearby; buggies and buckboards and such, and more horses, were parked behind the Grange.

Approaching the cowboy, York said, "Where you off to, Whit?"

The droopy-eyed, droopy-mustached foreman was walking his horse away, moving slow, but moving.

A touch of gruffness was in his voice. "Speechifyin' ain't my idea of a good time."

"No argument. Hold up there a second."

Murphy, reins in hand, brought his steed to a stop and faced the sheriff. "Not really in the mood to talk, York. I got things to do out at the Bar-O, and I had no urge to listen to such twaddle."

"What twaddle would that be?"

"Tearin' down Mr. Cullen's wishes while pretendin' to hold him up. Probably a big ol' picture of him'll be hangin' in that station, like he approved of the thing."

"Probably." York eased closer. "You know, Whit, we haven't had a chance to talk, you and me . . . since the O'Malley unpleasantness."

The foreman's eyes tightened to slits. "What's to talk about? Since when was you and I friendly?"

It was true that they'd had a run-in or two when York first came to town.

York said, "Thought you might be interested to know Burt O'Malley denied he ever had that set-to with the old man on the porch. The one you told me about? Oh, O'Malley said they argued some or, anyway, the talk got heated. But he claimed it was the night before, not that morning. And that it never came close to blows."

Murphy shrugged his narrow shoulders. "Who cares what that lyin' blackguard said? He hired that Preacherman to kill you, didn't he? Miss Willa says he confessed as much. She heard it from his own lips."

York nodded. "She did. I did. But the peculiar thing is, O'Malley never admitted to killing George Cullen, either accidentally or on purpose. To his very end, he said he loved the old man."

Murphy's lip curled into a sneer that lifted the droopy mustache on one side. "Funny way to show it. And a man who hires a gunman to kill another, he don't likely kill accidental."

York smiled just a little. "You know, generally I'd agree with you. But maybe O'Malley didn't do it. And maybe it *was* an accident."

The foreman was shaking his head and frowning. "You're not makin' sense, Sheriff. And I got better things to do than listen to such palaver."

Murphy seemed about to mount his horse when York's voice stopped him sharp. "*Whit*! There's something I haven't mentioned to Miss Willa. I found a mess of blood caked on a post on that porch. Human blood, Doc Miller says. Enough to show that somebody took a hell of a knock."

Reins still in hand, Murphy said, "That so?"

"It's so. I've taken that section of the post as potential evidence. Tucked it away in my safe. In there, as well, are pieces of bone collected just off the porch, near that post. Likely the doc could match them up to the hole in George Cullen's head, were we to dig him up. But that's as far as I've taken this so far."

Murphy snorted a humorless laugh. "Why bother? O'Malley's your man, and he's dead."

York's chin came up, and his gaze glared down. "Suppose it wasn't O'Malley that argued that morning with George Cullen. Suppose it was *you*, Whit."

The close-set eyes showed white all around. "You're out of your blasted mind, Caleb York! I *loved* that old man!"

York nodded. "So did Burt O'Malley. I believe you. But the old man wasn't the *only* one you loved out at the Bar-O, was he?"

"What the hell's that supposed to mean?"

"It means you've been yearnin' for Willa Cullen for a long, long time. Way before I got to town. And all that time you thought you were the son that George Cullen never had. You two were close—that's true enough. So close that maybe you thought the old man would be just fine with you marryin' his daughter and takin' over the Bar-O."

The eyes were slits again. "Careful what you say, York!"

"I generally am. For instance, I think that morning . . . the morning George Cullen died . . . you finally got it out in the open. Brought up a subject you figured would please the old man. Told him of your intentions, how you hoped to marry his daughter and keep the Bar-O a going concern."

The foreman was trembling with rage. "I've heard *enough* of this. . . ."

"But Cullen wasn't having any of it, was he? You were just some lowly cowboy he groomed into a decent foreman—a good hand, but not anybody good enough for his daughter. A man like George Cullen was the king of his little kingdom, and that made his daughter a princess. Some uppity trail hand wants to *wed* her? Ridiculous! Insulting. Even infuriating. Hell, the old boy may have started the fracas. I saw him do the same the night before, with Newt Harris. He'd been kinda erratic of late, ol' George. Being blind goes hard on a big man like that."

Jaw muscles pulsed at either edge of the thick mustache. "You best be careful what you say, York. What you do. You don't have a damn thing on me!"

"You didn't mean to kill him. You really did love that old man. But when he insulted you, belittled you, and then came at you with his fists up, you grabbed him and knocked him back. Slammed him a good one."

Murphy said nothing, but the trembling continued.

"Whit, you were the only one, really, who could've loaded the body up in a buckboard and staged that business with that chestnut of his. Like he ever would've been thrown by a gentle horse like that."

Murphy was shaking his head. "Can't prove nothin'. Not a damn thing."

York shrugged. "Maybe not. But somebody out at the Bar-O may have seen or heard somethin'. Lou Morgan, maybe, workin' the barn. Harmon in the cookhouse. Whole bunkhouse of cowhands."

The foreman snorted. "Anybody said anythin', they're damn liars."

"Oh, I haven't investigated yet. And I also haven't told Willa what I think. Once I do, though, you'll be finished at the Bar-O. She won't need any evidence. Just my say-so."

Murphy's hand hovered over his holstered .45.

York raised his left hand nice and easy. "Now, that's one way you can go, Whit. But would you please step away from that horse of yours? 'Cause my bullet might go through you, and I'd hate like hell to wound that animal."

Murphy slowly moved away from the horse, and York moved with him in a half circle.

"I suppose you might take me," York said, as if merely ruminating. "You never know in a gunfight. You might be the man to kill Caleb York. Stranger things have happened."

Now York was poised with his hand over the .44 in the low-slung holster.

"Or," York said, "you could saddle up, head out to the Bar-O, gather your things, and find somewhere else to be."

Murphy froze, hand still just above his holstered weapon. "And . . . and you'll tell Willa Cullen what?"

"That you got a letter from home and had to tend to things there."

"*What* things?"

"Why, you never said, Whit. You just told me you had family matters that needed seein' to. Your only job will be to never set foot in Trinidad again, or on the Bar-O. Give me your word on that, and I won't come looking for you. And I won't investigate further."

Murphy's smile was in the midst of a glare. "Why should I trust *you*?"

"Because I'm taking a risk, too. You see, I promised Willa I would kill the man who killed her father. If she finds out I just let that man ride off on his own, well, she might not look too kindly on that."

Murphy's right hand relaxed and slipped easily past the butt of his holstered gun. His shoulders slumped; he seemed unsteady on those cowboy bowed legs. His eyes were on the dusty earth.

"I did love that old man," he said softly, nothing gruff at all about it. "And . . . and Willa, too. Loved 'em both."

"I'm sure you did, Whit."

Murphy's grin was joyless. "Funny you should send me off sayin' it was a family matter."

"Yeah?"

"That old man and her, they was the only thing near a family as I ever had."

York had seen sadder things than the look in Murphy's eyes, but not many.

"Time for you to ride, Whit."

The former foreman of the Bar-O did just that. Climbed up and onto his horse and headed out, not fast, not slow. Never looking back.

York sighed and went over to sit on the short flight of steps to the Grange Hall. He waited till the building began to empty out, then gently wove his way through the exiting crowd back into the building, with many citizens patting him on the back and thanking him for his generosity. Of course, his action hadn't entirely been out of generosity—he and Parker would make a pretty penny off the Santa Fe for use of their depot.

He found Willa sitting on the stage, on one of the many hardwood chairs arranged there. Her hands were folded in her lap, and she looked very small, very young, in that feminine blue-and-white calico dress.

He sat beside her. "Big day."

She nodded.

"Your father might not be happy," he said.

She nodded.

York shrugged. "Might be ticked we didn't do things his way. But you're in charge now."

She nodded.

"I do think you're overdue, though," he said.

She looked at him.

He brushed a blond tendril from her forehead. "For those tears?"

She thought about that.

Then fell into his arms and wept.

Patting her on the back like a baby, Caleb York could only hope that she would agree with him if she ever put things together about Whit Murphy's sudden absence.

Agree that there were times when killing a man just wasn't the way.

About the Authors

MICKEY SPILLANE and MAX ALLAN COLLINS collaborated on numerous projects, including twelve anthologies, three films, and the *Mike Danger* comic book series.

Spillane was the bestselling American mystery writer of the twentieth century. He introduced Mike Hammer in *I, the Jury* (1947), which sold in the millions, as did the six tough mysteries that soon followed. The controversial PI has been the subject of a radio show, a comic strip, and several television series, starring Darren McGavin in the 1950s and Stacy Keach in the 1980s and 1990s. Numerous gritty movies have been made from Spillane novels, notably director Robert Aldrich's seminal film noir, *Kiss Me Deadly* (1955), and *The Girl Hunters* (1963), in which the writer played his own famous hero.

Collins has earned an unprecedented twenty-two Private Eye Writers of America "Shamus" nominations and won the award for the novels *True Detective* (1983) and *Stolen Away* (1993) in his Nathan Heller series, and for "So Long, Chief," a Mike Hammer short story begun by Spillane and completed by Collins. His graphic novel *Road to Perdition* is the basis of the Academy Award–winning film of the same name and starring Tom Hanks. A filmmaker in the Midwest, he has had half a dozen feature screenplays produced, including *The Last Lullaby* (2008), based on his innovative Quarry novels, also the basis of a Cinemax TV series. As "Barbara Allan," he and his wife, Barbara, write the "Trash 'n' Treasures" mystery series (recently *Antiques Frame*).

Both Spillane, who died in 2006, and Collins received the Private Eye Writers life achievement award, the Eye, and the Mystery Writers of America "Grand Master" Edgar Award.